MW00465181

For the Love of an Outlaw

(Outlaw Shifters, Book 1)

T. S. JOYCE

For the Love of an Outlaw

ISBN-13: 978-1985002753
ISBN-10: 1985002752
Copyright © 2017, T. S. Joyce
First electronic publication: November 2017

T. S. Joyce
www. tsjoyce.com

All Rights Are Reserved. No part of this book may be used or reproduced in any manner whatsoever without written permission, except in the case of brief quotations embodied in critical articles and reviews. The unauthorized reproduction or distribution of this copyrighted work is illegal. No part of this book may be scanned, uploaded or distributed via the Internet or any other means, electronic or print, without the author's permission.

NOTE FROM THE AUTHOR:

This book is a work of fiction. The names, characters, places, and incidents are products of the writer's imagination or have been used fictitiously and are not to be construed as real. Any resemblance to persons, living or dead, actual events, locale or organizations is entirely coincidental. The author does not have any control over and does not assume any responsibility for third-party websites or their content.

Published in the United States of America

First digital publication: November 2017
First print publication: February 2018

Editing: Corinne DeMaagd
Cover Photography: Wander Aguiar
Cover Model: Jonny James

DEDICATION

For you.

ACKNOWLEDGMENTS

I couldn't write these books without some amazing people behind me. A huge thanks to Corinne DeMaagd, for helping me to polish my books, and for being an amazing and supportive friend. Looking back on our journey here, it makes me smile so big. You are an incredible teammate, C!

Thanks to Jonny James, the cover model for this book and a few of my others. Any time I get the chance to work with him, I take it because he is so fun to work with. HavoK! Thank you to Wander Aguiar and his amazing team for this shot for the cover. You always get the perfect image for what I'm needing.

And last but never least, thank you, awesome reader. You have done more for me and my stories than I can even explain on this teeny page. You found my books, and ran with them, and every share, review, and comment makes release days so incredibly special to me.

1010 is magic and so are you.

ONE

Ava Dorset gritted her teeth and considered ignoring her brother's phone call. She knew him though, and if this was about the message he'd left two days ago, he wouldn't stop calling until she picked up.

Hand clenched tightly around the cell, she connected the call and answered, "No."

"Yes," Colton argued. "You owe me a lifetime of favors, and I've never called in a single one, and this is me, calling it in."

"I have a life, Colton. I can't just pick up and work for free. And it's not just the money either. Trigger makes me uncomfortable. He always has."

"You haven't seen him since high school, Ava, so

that argument is invalid. He's my best friend. Has been since we were kids, and you never gave him a chance—"

"Because there is something wrong with him! You get that, right? He's..." She didn't know how to explain how she felt, or about the bone-deep instinct that said Trigger was too cold, too empty, and his eyes... Ava swallowed hard and shook her head like Colton could see her. "I can't. I don't know what you're into, and I don't even want to know."

"Ava," Colton growled with a little too much grit to his voice. "One favor. I need you to sort out the financials on this place. Give me two weeks of your time and don't bullshit me with the money excuse. You have always been a saver, and I bet you haven't taken a day off work in five years. You owe me, and don't even make me remind you why. Come. Home." The line clicked. Ava tossed the phone onto the passenger's seat, gripped the wheel, and yelled a curse. It was her favorite curse and started with an F.

No one in the world could get under her skin like her older brother. Whatever people said about siblings being super-close had missed the mark big-time with the Dorset family. She lived on the other side of the country for a reason.

"Asshole," she muttered as she shoved open the door of her hybrid. Now she was going to have to take two weeks off right at the busiest time, right when her business was gaining momentum and poised to take off. Of course, Colton would surface just as she was on the verge of success. Her delinquent brother always mucked things up and didn't care about wasting anyone else's time as long as it suited his schedule.

This was Trigger's fault, too. That man was strange. And a criminal. Fine as hell from what she remembered, but her basic instincts said to steer clear of boys with empty eyes and rap sheets.

Colton was a fart-face, just like she'd nicknamed him growing up. In fact, if she really had to do this, she was bringing that box of embarrassing pictures of him and stapling them to telephone poles all over her hometown of Darby, Montana.

She hadn't been back here since age eighteen, the day after she graduated high school. Why? Because there was something wrong with the people of that town. She'd always been on the outside, unable to understand the dynamics, and there was nothing worse than feeling utterly alone in a place that was supposed to be "home."

Okay. Two weeks. She could do this, and then Colton could never hang anything over her head again. Her debt would be paid.

Two weeks, and she could get back to the life she was building.

Two weeks, and she would be right back here, and Colton and Trigger and the whole damn town would be in her rearview mirror again. And this time, it would be forever.

TWO

Trigger Massey swallowed hard and forced himself to look at the carnage. Dad had always told him not to look away from things that were hard to deal with. He'd told him from age three to accept the tough parts of his life. Own them. Get to a point where he could eventually revel in them, but he'd never quite gotten there. The scent of blood was still his least favorite smell in the world. Why? Because his life had been bathed in it.

Fourteen cattle, chewed up and left scattered across his south pasture. Fourteen. He calculated the money this cost him in his head, money he didn't have. Fuck. The worst part was he didn't know if they'd been killed by the local cougar clan as a warning, or if he'd done this. Sleep walker killer—that's what the monster inside of him turned him into.

"Come on," he murmured low, nudging Harley, his coal black work horse. The critter was big, sixteen hands high and intact, so the stallion was a handful on a good day. He fuckin' loved his pet monster. Mean as sin with the speed of a demon to match. A kindred spirit perhaps. If Trigger didn't get bitten or kicked five times a week, well, it was a slow week. The horse snorted and dragged his front hoof through the snow as if he was impatient after just thirty seconds of standing here. Spoiled beast. He wasn't bothered by the blood or the dead cattle, but he was bothered by not having a job to do. Sitting and thinking was Trigger's gig, not Harley's. He just wanted to run and terrorize the other horses and cause havoc.

Trigger heard Colton way before he saw him. That was the beauty of his extra senses. Perhaps it was one of the only benefits to the monster that raged inside of him. They were in the piney mountains of Montana, right on the edge of the continental divide. It was beautiful here, but on his property, there wasn't much open space. For a creature who relied on all senses, especially his sight, he needed to remedy that fast. He needed to rent some equipment and clear land, but with what money? Either his animal or the Darby Clan of mountain lion shifters was slaughtering his meager income.

"What?" he growled at Colton before he even turned around.

"Man, fuck you and your attitude today. I got you help."

"Don't need no help."

Colton pulled his bay horse up next to Harley and nearly got his mount kicked.

"You know better," Trigger gritted out, casting him a fiery glance. "Harley hates that horse."

"Harley hates every horse, and you never trained him to behave. Your fault."

"I like him mean."

"Ava's coming here."

When Trigger jerked with shock, Harley skittered to the side and snorted in agitation. His frozen breath blasted in front of him like freight train steam as he reared. Trigger yanked him back under control and kicked him, took off at a dead sprint, got him a hundred yards, and then circled back to Colton.

When he returned, Colton said, "He's the worst horse," as he leaned on his saddle horn and looked as bored as his horse with Harley's antics.

"Ava ain't welcome here."

"Why not?"

"Because she ain't!"

Colton's eyes flashed gold, and he sat up straight. "That ain't a good enough answer this time, Trigger. Explain why not!"

"Because she's a girl."

"This ain't fourth grade, and I'm not posting a no-girls-allowed sign on the front gate, you sexist dick!"

"It's not about being sexist, Colton! Have you told her? Huh?"

Colton didn't answer and turned away to hide the scars on his face.

"Hide them marks all you want from me. Won't stop me from thinking about them. Won't stop the guilt. You tell me all the time to get out of my head and stop thinking about what I did because you don't think about it. Lie. Big fuckin' lie."

"It ain't a lie! I came to grips with this five years ago, Trig."

"But you haven't told your baby sister what you are."

"That's the rules, right?" he yelled, lifting those fiery gold eyes to Trigger. When his face got red with fury, the scars looked even worse.

Don't look away, his dad's voice whispered in his mind. *Own the devil in you.*

Trigger wanted to puke off the side of his horse, but he made himself hold Colton's disfigured gaze. "Even if you had told her. Even if she knew what to expect when she saw you…" Trigger jammed a finger at the massacred cattle lying in stiff mounds in the thin snow. "How will you explain our lives to her? How will you explain the shit that keeps happening? We're in a damn freefall, and you're inviting a stranger to watch it."

"She's not a stranger, Trig. She's my sister."

"Who you let go."

"Because I had to." He gave Trig his profile, hiding the damn claw marks again. Colton swallowed hard and stared at the dead cattle with an unreadable expression. "Ava can stop our freefall."

Trigger snorted. "How?"

"She's good with money. She can tell us how to

11

save this place from the clan."

"It ain't savable."

"Fuck that. We aren't to the give-up part yet, Trig. You hate everyone and everything, right?" Colton flicked his fingers at the mountains. "You don't hate this place. It's your connection to your dad. Losing it can't happen. You'll truly be a monster if you do, and I ain't shooting you in the head, Trig."

"You swore—"

"I swore if it got to that point, but it ain't getting there! Ava will stop it!" Colton gritted his teeth, and a snarl ripped up his throat. His horse was used to that, just like Harley was, but the bay bounced to the side just the same. Colton gripped the reins and turned the horse in a tight circle once, then spat on the ground, eyes locked on Trigger's. "You made me into this, you sonofabitch. You don't get to leave me here alone to manage it. Fuck the clan. Fight everything. Ava will be here soon. Do yourself a favor and wash a fuckin' dish. She's not a laid-back woman. She'll give us hell, so prepare." Colton kicked his horse and bolted back in the direction of the barn.

"Fantastic!" Trigger yelled after Colton. "Like I'm not already in Hell!"

Stupid Colton. Ava couldn't stop anything. Trigger was a runaway freight train someone had set on fire. He had no brakes and had been rolling down a steep hill on greased tracks for years. There was no stopping his downfall. There was only slowing it down and dragging out the torture.

Therefore, he hated Ava just like he hated everyone else.

She wouldn't help.

Her good intentions would just make everything worse.

THREE

"Um, thank you for picking me up," Ava said as Cooper Langley turned off the switches in the small plane. It was a thirty minute drive to Darby from the tiny airport here.

He pulled his headset off his ears and placed them around his neck as he smiled at her. "My pleasure. Your dad was a good friend. Anytime you need a ride out here, you just let me know."

Dad wasn't good to anyone, so that was bullcrap. "Oh, this is the only time I'll need one. I didn't realize there aren't Uber drivers out here."

"Well, when your brother came to me a couple days ago and asked me to grab you, I have to admit I was surprised. You been gone so long, we thought you might never come back."

"We?"

The silver-haired grizzly of a man gave her a ghost of a smile and murmured, "The whole town. We don't lose many, but you couldn't seem to get out of Darby fast enough."

She frowned, utterly shocked that anyone had even noticed her absence. "Oh," she said lamely. "Well, I'm only back for a couple of weeks and then it's back to Alabama. That's my home."

"Home," he murmured mysteriously, and now Cooper wasn't smiling anymore. "Things have changed a bit since you lived here. Steer clear of the GutShot."

She scrunched up her face. That sounded gross. "What is the...GutShot?"

"A bar right in town. It's next to the antiques shop. Biker bar mostly, but the riffraff comes down from the mountains to blow off steam. It ain't that safe for fragile townies." Before she could react to the slight, he shoved open the door to the small five-seater plane and hopped out like he was a graceful antelope instead of a sixty-year-old arthritic man.

Ava scrambled out her side, highly offended. She

rounded the front of the plane, shouldering her purse better. "I'm not a fragile townie. I carry a knife. And I still know how to use it!"

"What the hell did you pack in here, woman?" Cooper complained as he wrestled her bright purple suitcase out of the storage hold. "Rocks and anvils and a pallet of bricks?"

"Ha ha. I'm here for two weeks. I brought enough so I don't have to use the laundromat."

Cooper snorted and set her suitcase on its wheels, pulled out the handle, and started dragging it toward an old Chevy parked beyond the landing strip of the small, private Trapper Creek Airport. "You're missin' out. Swampies Laundry is the social hub of the town now. You could learn all about the town you left behind in one good afternoon. They even serve little mini-bottles of wine while you wait for your clothes to dry. It's pretty dern highfalutin now. Perfect place for a lady like you to hang out." He cast her heeled booties a dirty look and then ignored her the rest of the way to his truck.

Ava sighed and checked the countdown on her phone. 326 more hours, and she could leave this place. Come on time, speed up!

The drive to town was filled with blaring country music and trying to figure out how to buckle the dilapidated seatbelt that kept coming undone in Cooper's truck. He drove the icy roads too fast for her liking, but he never slid off the side, so there was that. Darby was about the size of a cumquat, and likely she could hork a piece of gum from one side of the town to the other. And she wasn't even a practiced spitter.

Being a small town meant every inch of it was full of old memories she thought she'd buried. How many times had she eaten biscotti cookies in the coffee shop after school with her friend Moira and voiced their dreams of leaving this place? How many makeshift football games had she joined in the field behind Jody's Pizza Shack? How many times had she wandered out to the park on Main Street and sat in the swings in the middle of the night, contemplating all the changes she wanted in her life? How many bowling nights with Dad before he left, and movie nights with herself, had she done right here on the main drag in Darby? How many times had she gotten into fights with her brother after Dad left and Colton tried to control everything she did? How many times had she yelled, "You aren't my father!" when Colton tried to get her to stay here after senior year? How many times had she been angry he didn't understand her need to leave? How many times had she been furious he wanted to keep her where she hurt the most?

And what had he done? Dragged her right back here. Typical.

He was only three years older than her, but had always tried to control her life. She wasn't a woman who gave up control, though. Not without one helluva fight. Dad had always said, "Fight everything." He said it most when he was preparing to leave them, but it had left a lasting impression. And so she did. She fought everything, and so far, it had worked. She was unattached to anyone and building her own little mini empire. No one could touch her, hurt her, or have any control over her life. Sure, it was lonely, but it was better than the alternative. She wasn't a girl who did well in a cage.

Darby was a cage.

"Here we are," Cooper muttered, slowing. He eased to a stop in front of the entrance of Two Claws Ranch. She only knew it was because of the dilapidated wooden sign that arched above the snowy road.

"Where's here?" she asked.

"This is as far as I go. You wanted to see Trigger Massey? He lives here. Inherited the place when his pa died a few years back. He's doing a pretty fair job of running it into the ground. It's impressive actually." Cooper's tone had changed. It was lower, gravelly, and he wouldn't look at her. He gripped the wheel and his body hummed with such tension, the fine hairs on the back of her neck lifted.

"Your dad wouldn't have wanted you hanging around the likes of him, just so you know. Whatever you're doing here, get your business done quick and come back to town. Triple Creek has rooms open, and it's real comfortable."

"Yeah? Is it a place my dad would approve? Do me a favor, Cooper. Don't talk about what my dad would and wouldn't want. I knew him best, and he was fine with Trigger. Thanks for the ride."

Whoa, what had made her say that? She'd just stuck up for Trigger Massey. The scary boy from her school days. Before she could pop-off anymore, she shoved the creaking truck door open and dragged the suitcase out of the back. She wasn't usually rude to people, but what he'd said made her angry for reasons she couldn't figure out.

"Call me if you need anything," Cooper said out the window, and then his truck was blasting down the road away from her, the exhaust billowing smoke behind it.

Ava watched the old truck until it disappeared around a bend in the road, and then she zipped up her too-thin jacket, pulled her winter hat down lower over her ears, and began dragging her suitcase down the snowy road of Two Claws.

She tried to call Colton as she struggled and slipped up the lane, but her phone was getting zero service out here. Great. She didn't even know if Colton was here, and she suddenly grew nervous about meeting Trigger alone.

Why hadn't she packed snow boots? These booties really were the most impractical shoes to wear out here, but she'd been living down south for so long where winters were mild, she hadn't worn snow boots in years. She would need to go to town and buy some tomorrow, and perhaps a thicker jacket too.

It felt like she walked for three days, and hell yep,

she was muttering curse words the entire way because, really, things couldn't get much worse. She was freezing, and this road went on for twenty-five miles for all she knew, and it was getting darker by the minute. The roiling storm clouds above decided to poop snow right as she was kicking herself for giving into Colton's request to come here, and as the fat snowflakes fell down around her, she stopped, chest heaving with breath, and glared up at the sky. Mother Nature was being a heifer with her timing.

When Ava looked at the road again, there was movement from far off. She squinted her eyes, but it was hard to see clearly through the falling snow. Something large approached, closer and closer until she could make out the edges of a black horse and a man riding it straight-backed and proud. He wore a cowboy hat pulled low over his eyes, a blue plaid shirt, but no jacket, like the weather didn't bother him at all. And as his horse closed the last ten yards, it began prancing and snorting, trotting sideways toward her, his eyes rolling and wild. The man atop the black horse didn't seem concerned, and when he lifted his chin, she could see his face better.

She hadn't thought about Trigger Massey in a

long time before Colton called her, but by God, he sure looked different from when he was a kid. He was the same age as Colton, so thirty-one now. His beard was thick and black, and his eyes matched the ebony color. His nose had been broken and healed slightly crooked, though it suited his rigid features. His dark hair was shaved short on the sides under his cream-colored cowboy hat, and there were tattoos up his neck and on both hands. She could only assume he was covered with ink on his arms as well. There was no welcoming smile or hint of kindness in his sparking eyes. Only annoyance dwelled in his features. That part she completely recognized. That part hadn't changed one bit in the ten years since she'd left Darby behind.

"You need better shoes," he said in a deep voice. "Would've taken you half the time to get to the cabin."

"I'm aware. Thank you."

"And probably a better jacket, too. This place ain't a high fashion runway. No one gives a shit what you look like here."

Well, this was going about as bad as it could go. With an angry glare, she dragged her suitcase through the snow and marched past him. "I'm here as a favor," she said over her shoulder. "You could at least pretend to be polite."

"I didn't call in any favors, and you don't owe me anything."

"No, but Colton did, and I owe him plenty. Unfortunately." God, it was cold out here.

She stumbled over a rock that had been hidden by the snow and nearly fell.

"Here," Trigger said from way too close.

Ava nearly jumped out of her skin when he took the suitcase handle from her. What the hell? He had been up on the horse, and then one second later he was down beside her, offering to take the suitcase. That man was scary fast and agile.

"I can get it myself," she said, gripping the handle tighter.

Trigger narrowed his eyes and stood to his full height. Holy macaroni, the man had grown half a damn foot since she'd seen him last and was now as wide as a creek. His shoulders were powerful and pressed against his flannel shirt, and his neck was thick with muscle. He was sexy as sin, but the devil was in his eyes, and a wise woman didn't muck with a dangerous man like him. He took a step closer, and then another, until his chest nearly brushed hers. He looked down his nose at her, then bent forward. She honestly didn't know if he was going to kiss her or kill her. It took everything she had to stand her ground. He yanked the suitcase handle out of her hand and leaned in closer, his lips right near her ear. "I'm not gonna watch you struggle this damn frilly suitcase another quarter mile just because you're being a stubborn woman. Get on the horse. It's supper time and I'm hungry, and having you here pisses me off. Pop off less, and we'll get along just fine."

"You mean don't talk."

Trigger straightened his spine and angled his face. "Your words, not mine, but I don't disagree."

"You're still an asshole."

He gave her an empty, careless smile. "Guilty. Get on the horse, Ava, before I lose my patience and leave you out in the snow."

She hated him. Hated him for being just the same as he was, hated him for bossing her around first thing, hated him for trying to intimidate her. She matched his empty smile and flipped him the bird, and then she did an about-face and marched through the snow without looking back.

She was pretty sure he growled when he passed her on the horse, her luggage dangling to the side like it didn't weigh anything at all, but she didn't care about his man-tantrums. He was pissed off she was here? She felt the same!

Dick-weevil-anal-fungus-meathead. Probably hung like a gerbil, and too mean for girls to like past his pretty face, so he was just bitter and angry and— and—sexually frustrated enough that he had tricked himself into thinking he was some kind of demigod who could order people around. Well, not her. No siree-bob. Maybe his rugged good looks made some girls fall over themselves to mind him, but she would rather chew off her own leg than be bossed around by the likes of him. He'd been rude when they were kids, and he was just as rude now. There was something very disappointing about a man who refused to improve with time.

What Colton saw in him as a friend, she would never in a million years figure out.

It took her a good fifteen minutes before she reached the front of a small cabin. She was cold, huffing breath, exhausted, and in a foul mood, but at least when she shoved the door open, the innards of the house were warm and her suitcase was sitting in the middle of the small entryway. It would've taken her a lot longer to get here if she was dragging that dang thing through the snow the whole time. And bright side number three, Trigger was nowhere in sight. It smelled like food, and her brother was standing with his back to her in a modest kitchen with wooden counters that matched the cabinets.

"Why didn't you pick me up from the airport?" she asked. That part still stung. Yeah, they didn't get along, but he could've shown a little care.

With a sigh, Colton braced his arms against the counter and said, "Because I didn't want to have this moment in public."

"What moment?"

He turned around, slowly, and locked his attention on her, but she could only stare in horror at the mangled and scarred left side of his face. Deep claw marks were etched into his cheek, from his temple all the way to his jawline. The marks just barely missed his eye.

"Oh, my gosh," she whispered, dropping her purse where she stood. "What happened to you?"

"Bear attack."

"When?" she said much too loudly.

He winced and hunched his shoulders. "Five years ago."

"And you decided to never tell me?"

"Well, I lived, didn't I? And there wasn't much to tell. I got attacked, I survived, you weren't around to see the scars, so what was the point?"

"God, we're so broken," she murmured, tears burning her eyes. "So terribly broken." And she realized in that moment she hadn't really had a family since she'd left. She'd been on her own, Colton had been on his own, and they'd built totally separate lives. And there was tragedy in that, even if they didn't get along. She should've known if something this horrific had happened to him. And how many things about her life had she kept from him? Most of them. She barely even recognized her own brother. Even his eyes looked a different color from what she remembered.

She'd failed him, he'd failed her, and it shouldn't have been like this.

"I'm glad you're finally back," he said gruffly, running his hand over his short, dirty-blond hair. "I wanted you to come before..." He swallowed hard. "Well, all I mean is I wished you came sooner."

"I didn't mean for that either." She felt the need to explain. "It's just, I wanted to leave here so badly, and I didn't want to come back that first year. I didn't want to get sucked back in. I wanted a shot at building an existence outside of here. And the longer I was away and the less contact with this town I had, the easier it was and the less I thought about..."

"Me," Colton murmured.

Ava's stomach curdled, and she was too ashamed to say the truth, so she dipped her gaze to the scraped-up wooden floors instead.

"It's all good, Ava. We can both beat ourselves up, but what will that fix? Nothing. Do you want one can or two?"

"What?" she asked, confused.

"One can of ranch-style beans or two. Me and Trig usually eat four apiece."

"You eat canned beans? For a whole meal?"

"Well, not just canned beans. We add steak to them, too. Look." He forked a steaming sirloin from the pan on the stove and smiled. Only the scarred side of his face wouldn't allow a grin on that side, so his expression was crooked. "You can call them something fancier if you want. We're serving edible squish-pebbles, Princess. One or two cans?"

"Um. One. Can of...beans. Would be nice. Thank you." Kind of. *Note to self: get snow boots, warmer jacket, and adult food from the store tomorrow.*

"If you want to put your suitcase away, Trig has a guest room down there." Colton gestured toward a hallway off the living room and went back to cooking.

"Wait, I'm staying here? With Trigger? I thought I would stay with you."

"Well, I'll be right out the door and about a hundred yards west of this cabin, but my place is just one room. You will be more comfortable here."

"With Trigger Massey?" she asked in a dead voice.

"Yes, with Trig. Ava, he's good. You're safe here. Trust me."

"Like you were safe?" she asked quietly.

"I told you it was a bear attack. What do you want me to do about that? They aren't really in any man's control. They happen. I got lucky. I lived." But his tone had gone dark midway through, and he didn't sound like he believed the lucky part. "Go on, put your things away. Dinner will be ready in a few minutes."

"Okay," she murmured, grabbing the handle to her suitcase. He'd dismissed her, and normally she would've fought it, but Colton was really different than she remembered. A few minutes by herself to process everything was probably a good idea.

She would've been careful dragging the wheels across wooden floors, but these were all banged up, and a few more scrapes and scratches would only add to the rustic character. The first bedroom had a king-sized bed with a frame made out of polished, natural, knotty wood. There was a huge dream catcher hanging above the bed, and the top drawers on the small dresser were open...and full. The comforter on the bed was forest green and all disheveled like it hadn't been made in a long time. She couldn't judge Trigger though, since she hadn't made her own bed in a month. What was the point? She never invited anyone over.

Farther down the hallway was a bathroom and one smaller bedroom about the size of a large closet. There was a twin bed in there and a small space to walk to get to it, but that was it. There was barely even room to set her suitcase on the floor, so she hefted it onto the bouncy, squeaking mattress instead.

"There wasn't enough room for a dresser," a gruff voice said from behind her.

With a yelp, Ava jumped and clutched her chest, as if that would keep her heart from pounding right out of it.

Trigger reached right over her like he had no concept of personal space and pulled a cord on the wall. A set of three shelves released with a click. "I built these."

"O-okay."

He didn't budge, just stood there, looking down at her from mere inches away.

He lifted his gaze to the ceiling and clasped his hands behind his back. "I'll get girl-food tomorrow."

"Girl food," she repeated.

"Yeah. Salad and fruit and shit."

"Well shit sounds disgusting, but salad and fruit would be good." She let off a nervous laugh, but he didn't seem amused by her poop joke. Great, he didn't have a sense of humor either. These next two weeks were going to be super-fun.

He rocked from his toes to his heels to his toes again, then lowered his gaze to hers. "It'll storm again tonight."

"But the weather report said—"

"It's wrong. Trust me."

"Okay then." Psychopath. "Sooo, I think I should get to work on your finances after dinner." If one could call canned beans dinner.

He nodded curtly. "The faster you get through it, the faster you can leave."

She gave a too-bright smile. "Exactly. If you could gather your taxes from the last three years, any investments, retirement accounts, a detailed list of debts and credit card balances, as well as a list of monthly expenses, that would be extremely helpful." She pulled a folded spreadsheet out of her bag. It had lines for expenses and a questionnaire so she could get to know what kind of spender he was. "Also, I need paperwork on all streams of revenue you have coming in. And I'll need access to your bank accounts. You can either give me read-only access or give me the passwords to your online bank accounts."

"That's pretty invasive, don't you think?"

"If you're worried about me stealing all your money, don't be. I'm a professional, and if you had money to steal, I wouldn't be here. You can change your password the second I'm finished assessing the damage."

His dark eyes narrowed to slits. "Great."

"Fantastic."

"Steller," he muttered.

"Super-dee-duper."

The corner of his lips twitched into the ghost of a smile, but disappeared so fast that, for a moment, she thought she imagined it. In all the time she'd known him, she'd never once seen Trigger Massey smile. But that split second of a amused expression had completely changed his features. He could be a dashing man, not just dangerous looking, if he let that slip more often. She should encourage it.

"You have a nice smile," she said.

Trigger narrowed his eyes and his nostrils flared slightly as he sniffed the air. "Beans are on." And then he did an about-face and left her there with her mouth hanging open.

Okay then.

She took a test sniff of the air too, but she didn't smell anything but the faint aroma of sawdust. Maybe he had just built the shelves.

She gave her attention to the fold-down shelves

and ran her fingers across the top. No dust. In fact, the entire room was spotless, and the sheets and comforter had been folded neatly at the end of the bed for her to put on fresh. It was better than she'd expected from a bachelor.

Not in a big rush to devour beans, she unpacked her suitcase and even set her make-up and other toiletries on the counter in the small bathroom next to her room. God, this was uncomfortable. She couldn't believe she was in Trigger's house, much less staying here for two weeks. This was what nightmares were made of.

"Ava, hurry up! We're waiting on you!" her brother called from the other room.

Annoying. Plus, if she was honest, she was stalling. This place was homey, but it wasn't home, and she was missing her little efficiency apartment. She should be home right now, sipping hot chocolate, playing an old record in the background, and working on all the stuff she hadn't gotten done at the office. Not in the wilderness, not in the hometown she never wanted to revisit, with some hot, but unnerving, weirdo who was light on manners and heavy on fiery looks, silence, and awkwardness.

"Oh my God, Ava!" Colton called. "You don't need to put make-up on or fix your hair. This ain't the Ritz, and no one here cares what you look like. I'm hungry, and my food is getting cold! You know what is worse than anything in the whole motherfuckin' world? Cold food. One foot after the other. Let's go."

If Trigger Massey didn't murder her in her sleep, Colton was going to drive her to jump off a cliff. Either way, the next two weeks were getting bleaker by the second.

Barely resisting the urge to stomp down the hallway like she had when she was a teenager when Colton pissed her off, she glided gracefully into the living room with a plastered smile on her face. But where she'd expected a pair of giant, tatted-up cowboy behemoths, Colton was the only one sitting at the counter on a rickety old stool that didn't match the other two. He was shoveling beans into his maw from a can. He slurped a stray edible squish-pebble, as he'd so eloquently called it, and around that bite of food he said, "I quit waiting on you."

"Obviously." She looked around the room, at the taxidermy moose head over the stone fireplace, the mismatched, ancient leather couches, and knitted bear pillows that sat in disarray on the cushions. There was a coat rack, but it only hung one jacket. "Where's Trigger?" she asked nonchalantly.

"Don't get a crush on that man." Colton's voice had gone so serious she spun and stared at him. His eyes looked strange. It bothered her she didn't recognize his eyes anymore. The smile lines had disappeared from his face completely. He didn't look like the good-humored brother she had left all those years ago. Right now, he looked different. He looked...fierce. Intimidating. Harsh.

"I don't have a crush," she murmured. "He's not my type."

"What's your type these days, sis? Because I remember you liked a challenge in school. You liked them bad boys." He jammed his spoon at the front window. "That mess is on a whole different level. He just got out of jail for the third time, Ava. You're safe in this house, but don't let yourself get attached to that man. You understand?"

Trigger was out on the front porch on a swing, elbows on his knees, looking down at where his hands cupped a can of food. He rocked gently. His head jerked once, twice, like he had a twitch, and his lips moved as if he was talking to himself.

Unable to take her eyes from him, she asked softly, "What did he go to jail for?"

"Fighting."

"Fighting who?"

"The whole damn town." Colton held her gaze a moment longer, then gave her his back and returned to eating. She'd been dismissed. Sometimes he reminded her so much of their dad. Just the memory of him made her feel hollow inside. She hated it here. She'd worked so hard to bury thoughts of her past, but this town was full of ghosts. Full of memories. Full of regrets and things she never wanted to think about again.

With a sigh, she approached the counter and sank onto a wooden stool on the end. With a flick of his fingers, Colton slid a silver can down the counter that landed directly in front of her. He was a lot smoother than she remembered. The tin can had one of those plastic sporks sticking out of it that made her think the boys had been getting their disposable dinnerware from the fast food restaurants in town. They were basically thirty-one-year-old frat boys.

She exhaled air and then began to eat her dinner

slowly. It wasn't bad, thanks to the steak, and it was still hot. Ava wouldn't admit it out loud, but it did hit the spot after the snowy walk in. And thanks to her stomach being warmed up and the fireplace heating her outsides, she stripped out of her jacket about midway through dinner. The disgusted sound she made when she noticed Colton scarfing his fourth can down was a complete accident. He didn't seem to care though, since his only response was, "I have to eat a lot more now."

"I don't understand where you physically put that much food," she muttered, eyeing his big arms and trim waist. He looked so different than her jovial older brother who'd always slapped at his belly and joked he liked having a keg, not a six pack. "So you're a gym rat now?"

"I don't go to a gym."

"Do you have work-out equipment here?"

"Nope."

"You take steroids?" she asked, annoyed at his shortness.

"Also nope. This is just how I'm built."

"This ain't genetics, Colton. Dad was five-foot six and built like Santa Claus. If you don't want to tell me about your life, okay. I'm just trying to make small talk."

"You want to get to know me again? Here's something real. I waited for you to come back here, Ava. I've been here the whole time. You're the only family I got, and you never came home. Not once, until I called in favors and begged you here. I'm mad. I'm fired up. Where were you?"

"You know where I was. I was building a life outside this place."

"No, not physically, Ava. I mean where were you when I needed you? You could've answered my calls. Could've called me back. Hell, you could've texted me every once in a while just to let me know you were okay. A postcard? Christmas card? Birthday card? Anything, and I would've pinned it to the damn fridge." He jerked his chin toward the refrigerator, black to mismatch the stainless-steel stove. On it was a single picture under a magnet that was shaped like a bear claw. It was a black and white photograph of them sitting beside each other at a high school football game. She'd been mid-sentence, mouth open with whatever she was saying to the photographer, and Colton was looking over at her with a grin on his face as if she was telling a joke. The edges of the picture were tattered, like someone had handled it a lot.

What was this feeling? This ripping sensation in her chest? The hollowness inside of her was filling with something even more uncomfortable. Guilt?

She swallowed the bite in her mouth, but it felt like cement going down. "I should've called more."

Colton's blond brows lifted high over his muddy, goldish-green eyes. "Yeah, Ava. You should've."

She pursed her lips and rested her cheek on her palm, her elbow on the natural wood counter. "I'm sorry," she murmured, holding his gaze. "I really am."

Colton froze, and for a few seconds, they just stayed like that, staring at each other, two almost-strangers, made that way by the canyon of years that stood between them. Clearly, they were both very different than when they'd been in the same room last.

Colton shook his head and made a ticking sound. "It's okay. Don't worry about it."

It was a throwaway response, so to ease the tension she loaded a straggler bean onto her spork and launched it at him like a tiny catapult. It bounced off his smooth cheek, and he slid her a narrow-eyed glare.

"Forgive me," she demanded. "Say it."

He snarled up his lip as she fingered another bean onto her spork. "Say it," she told him.

Colton ducked neatly out of the way of the next flying bean. "Stop it, you little monster," he growled. "I forgive you. Whatever. It's not like I really gave you much thought after you left. You were always annoying as hell. Apparently, that hasn't changed. Now I'm glad you didn't come back here."

"I think you mean witty, entertaining, and gracious."

Colton snorted. "More like obnoxious, conceited, and exhausting."

"That's not polite."

Colton tilted his head back and emptied the rest of the contents of the can into his mouth. Well, his manners were exactly the same, so there was that.

She glanced over her shoulder at the front porch where Trigger was still rocking gently on the swing, but this time he wasn't talking to himself. He was staring right back at her, and his eyes looked so strange. They were a pretty gold color in this lighting, and his dark brows were furrowed slightly as though trying to figure her out.

She gestured him inside to eat with them, but Trigger stood suddenly and made his way down the porch stairs and into the snowy yard. His boots left deep prints as he strode deliberately to the woods and disappeared into the shadows. Okaaay.

"Number one rule of the house," Colton said in a gritty voice. "Don't leave the cabin at night."

"Why not?"

Colton slid a narrow-eyed glare at the place where Trigger had walked into the woods. The light above them made the scars on his face shine. "Because the predators come out at night."

FOUR

This was the part that would haunt him tomorrow.

Trigger shrugged out of his plaid button-down shirt and yanked the white T-shirt underneath over his head. He chucked both of them at a tree, pissed the bear was asking to rip out of him again so soon. He'd Changed last night in preparation for Ava's arrival so he should've had at least another week before he needed to do this. And what was he fuckin' doing? Night one, and she was calling the animal out.

This right here was why he'd hated being around her when they were kids.

She made the bear worse.

And now he knew exactly what kind of torture it

felt like to Turn someone. A friend. He'd lost his mind and tried to kill Colton, his best friend, and now look at his life. Trigger had completely ruined Colton's future. And if he wasn't careful, he was going to ruin Ava's, too. Or worse. The bear would just kill her.

Fuck, this was a terrible idea. A growl rumbled through his core as the animal disagreed. The beast liked blood too much for his own damn good. And by the way the bear had studied the dead cattle the other day, he must've killed them. It wasn't the Darby Clan of mountain lions that had done that. He had no one to blame but himself. Trigger, the man, had no memory of doing it, but he'd slaughtered part of his own herd. Those cows had the perfect telltale grizzly kill marks. Claws deep down either side of the spine and deep bite marks right beside them. He hunted them and grabbed them from behind. That was his move. More cattle lost, more money lost, and Ava was going to see just how badly he'd screwed himself into the ground. A wave of shame washed over him and brought on a crippling slash of pain through his middle.

With a grunt, he fell to his bare knees in the snow. He didn't even feel the cold. All he felt was the ache of the animal, the sickness of the insanity that was about to take him, the tingling of his skin as it prepared to rip apart and re-form as something *other*. As a monster.

Dad always called the grizzly a gift, but he'd been wrong.

He was a curse.

Natural born shifters were males. All of them. Females didn't make good monsters, but males...well, they suited the animal.

If he bit Ava, she could Turn, sure. But would she survive that first Change? Probably not. He'd watched Colton bleed out and stop breathing. Crimson had soaked the snow. Five years ago, he'd killed the human part of his friend, and still, half a decade later, he couldn't get the vision of Colton's dead eyes staring up at the stars. Or the memory of the exact second they turned from blue to gold. Curse.

Ava needed to do her job and get the hell out of here and away from Trigger as soon as possible.

Another wave of pain slammed through him, and the snap of bones sounded in the night as his spine busted and reshaped. *Pop, pop, pop!* Trigger gritted his teeth and tried like he always did to die quietly.

Because that's what this was, right? His human had to die so that the bear could live for a night.

Ava was so goddamn beautiful. She didn't even know it either. She never had. Trigger bowed over as his arm bones snapped. He clung to the memory of her face. He shouldn't, he knew. It was dangerous to let the bear see her, but he couldn't help it. He wanted to think of something beautiful while he died.

She had short, black hair that she curled up pretty. It was shiny like raven's feathers. She used to wear it long, but not anymore. He liked it better now. She looked tough. Pretty and tough. He imagined her profile when she'd smiled at Colton when they were eating. He hadn't been able to stop watching her. The faces she made. God, she was so animated he could read every emotion she ever had just in her eyes alone. He'd witnessed guilt, regret, hope, and relief on her face tonight. Oh, he'd heard their conversation. Heard Colton call her out for not coming home. Watched her react. Pretty, short, raven-colored curls and dark lashes that brushed her rosy cheeks when she looked down. Blue eyes, but not a stormy blue. They were icy blue, like Colton's used to stay. She had a round pixie face and full lips that always looked pouty. She wore red lipstick like she never expected to kiss a man. Perfectly arched dark eyebrows that told him exactly how she was feeling at any given moment.

He'd watched her like a damn hawk when they were younger, and she hadn't changed that much in all these years. Maybe she was even prettier now. Curvier. Softer with an hourglass figure he wanted to grab and own. Maybe she was even more animated. More independent for sure, but that was sexy. Ava didn't need anyone in the whole world, and all that did was make Trigger more interested in observing her. Dangerous game.

"Fuck," he gritted out as his body broke.

Pretty Ava. Pretty face, but as the bear took him, an awful image came to his mind. Colton's face morphed to hers, and her pretty face...her perfect, porcelain skin...was marred by the horrific scars that her brother now bore—Trigger's claw marks.

This was why he couldn't have pretty things. Why he couldn't have delicate things. Ava was tough for a human, but next to him, she was still a hummingbird. Pretty to look at, enthralling, but one touch from him and she would be nothing.

And he couldn't shoulder anymore guilt than he already did.

So just like when he was a kid, he told himself the mantra that made him leave her alone.

She deserves a normal life, and you destroy everything. For once, do something good. Leave that girl alone.

And then the bear exploded out of him with a horrific and triumphant roar, and in the seconds before Trigger ceased to exist, he prayed like always that the bear would stay away from the cabin.

FIVE

Okay, Ava was officially worried about Trigger. Colton had gone to his little cabin right before the snow hit, but now it had turned into a blizzard. Trigger had been right earlier about the storm. This was white-out bad, though, and he still wasn't back inside.

She thought she saw movement and squinted out the front window, but nope, it was just more snow. Crap. Maybe she should call the police. Colton had promised her he was fine, but the windchill had it way below freezing, and how could he see in this weather? Maybe Trigger was lost or hurt.

Not that she cared.

No, scrap that, she did care. He was a person.

Even if he was rude and weird, she didn't wish him dead by hypothermia, a broken leg in a blizzard, or getting eaten by a bear or a wolf pack, or a mountain lion, or something. There were a lot of ways to die out here.

She should definitely call the police. Ava shoved off the couch by the front window and motored down the hallway, her rainbow-colored fuzzy socks slipping and sliding on the wood floors in her hurry. She'd forgotten to pack her dang pajama pants, so she was currently wearing a tank top, fuzzy socks, a pair of bright red panties and a robe that she had kept tightly tied around herself just in case Trigger came back in unexpectedly. Right now, though…she had this awful feeling in her gut he wasn't coming back to his cabin at all, so she didn't care that the hem of her robe flapped behind her as she made her way into her room and ripped the cell phone off the charger.

Zero bars, zero service, and even standing on the bed, she couldn't get a call out. Crappity-crap.

What should she do?

Plan A: Bolt onto the porch and yell his name so he could find the cabin through the snow.

Boom. Survivalist.

Ava made her way to the porch, remembered belatedly about Colton's warning about predators, did an about-face, grabbed an iron poker from the fireplace, and stood on the front porch heaving panicked breaths. And then she sucked that frigid mountain air into her lungs and yelled Trigger's name as loud and as long as she could. Three seconds between sets, and she was yelling again. And again. And again. Until her throat was raw and scratchy.

Maybe she should walk to Colton's cabin and get him to help. She scrunched up her face and tried to make out Colton's small one-room house through the blizzard, but she couldn't see three feet off the front porch. It would be so easy to get turned around and lost. Trigger was no Romeo, and she sure as shit wasn't Juliette, so she wasn't dying with him tonight.

He was weird, but he was also super-hot, and the shallow, horny part of her thought it was sad the world would have one less hunk in it after tonight. Geez, what was wrong with her?

"Trigger!" she screamed again in a hoarse voice.

"Did Colton not tell you the house rule?" Trigger growled from right beside the porch.

Ava shrieked and skittered to the side, clutching

her chest.

Trig was butt-naked, and holy hell, his dick was glorious. And huge. And half hard. She stared at his nethers like the cool girl she was, and that made her mad because she'd been out here trying to save his life and now he was dick-stracting her from her fury. That was messed up!

"Where the devil did you come from? I've been looking for you! I thought you were hurt or dead or something. And you're—you're naked!" Her voice jacked up an octave. "Why are you naked?"

He uncrossed his arms and pushed off the railing he'd been leaning on and gestured to her torso. "I could also ask why you are immodestly dressed out in a snow storm, but I'm sure you have a good reason."

Ava looked down at the open front of her robe, spied the red of her panties, and squeaked as she rushed to pull the robe around her like a tortilla on a burrito. "I was worried. And not concerned with how I was dressed." And apparently not cold.

His eyes were glued to her crotch-region, so she kicked at the air and stabbed the log poker at him. "Eyes up here, Massey."

"Are those rainbow socks?" he asked.

Ava was trying not to look at his body, truly she was, but Trigger's chest was covered in tattoos, and he had a six pack that flexed with every frozen breath. His arms were huge, his legs powerful, and her earlier uncharitable thoughts about him being hung like a gerbil were completely, one-hundred-percent untrue. "Big dick," she muttered before she could stop herself.

Trigger offered her a slow, devil-may-care smile and said, "Eyes up here, Dorset."

Panicked, she dropped the log poker on the porch and muttered, "Righty-oh," like a weirdo, turned on her heel, and bolted into the house. "I'm glad you lived," she yelled over her shoulder as she speed-walked down the hall to the tiny guest bedroom.

Panting and her cheeks on fire, she slammed the door and stood in the crevice between the bed and the wall, eyes so wide she felt the need to blink four times in a row. Her mouth hung open as she remembered his big, perfect dick.

Trigger was a cowboy-boot-wearing Adonis. He was the perfect specimen of male. Cocky man with cut musculature that he obviously spent a great deal of time sculpting in the gym, tattoos that were perfectly chosen and placed, and the gold in his eyes was downright sexy, and less terrifying now for some reason.

No, no, no. Don't get a crush. It's Trigger. Trigger Massey. The boy who was always rude and could barely stand to look at you. That is not your person. Leave that boy alone.

The door swung open, and as she jumped in startlement, Trigger strode in, fastening a belt buckle over some jeans he'd put on. He was still shirtless, and his eyes were locked right on hers with such an intensity in them, her stomach dipped to her toes. His black hair was mussed on top as though he'd run his big hands through it, and there was a devilish smile sitting right at the corners of his lips. He didn't say a word, just shoved her robe off her shoulders, gripped her waist, and dragged her against him. His skin was surprisingly hot. She knew because she splayed her palms against his chest, and that heat zinged straight up her arms. His chest was hard as a rock, and her breath began to shake. She should run. Every instinct from her childhood said this was a bad idea, but the way he grabbed her with such confidence made her want to give in. Something about the sparking intensity in his eyes as he searched her face made her want to give him control. How utterly terrifying. How utterly exciting.

He slid his hand up her waist, dragging the hem of her tank top along with it, fingertips brushing her bare skin as he slid her shirt upward. Her body quivered and warmed from the inside out in anticipation. It had been so damn long since a man had touched her. Since she'd allowed anyone to touch her.

She exhaled a soft, shaking breath. "Trigger," she whispered.

A strange sound emanated from his throat. It was almost as if he purred. It was a sexy noise, and his fingertips found her jawline. He brushed it in gentle strokes, like he was petting her. Like he was steadying her, and then he gritted his teeth in a feral smile and gripped her jaw. She yelped, but he only angled his face and seized her lips with his. It was rough. His beard scratched her soft skin, and his teeth grazed her lips. Three seconds, and he pushed his tongue past her lips and tasted her. *Run. Run Ava, what are you doing?* But her feet were planted and now her traitor hands were sliding up his chest and wrapping around the back of his neck.

She didn't want him to stop. Since she'd come here, she'd been bombarded with memories she'd long ago buried, but Trigger was giving her an escape from all the noise in her head. With each stroke of his tongue, she lost herself a little more. And she didn't hate it. In fact...she liked it.

She brushed her tongue against his, and that purring sound emanated from his chest again. She could feel it against her breasts now that he'd pulled her in close. His arm was strong around her back now, his other hand holding her face in place as he kissed her like no man had done before. It was wild, powerful, and unexpected, and each time he changed the angle of his head, he never left her lips. It was as if he liked the taste of her so much he couldn't bear to put an inch between them for even a moment.

Traitor body backed slowly toward the bed, testing him, and Trigger followed, his body staying right with hers. It was graceful and easy, like a dance they'd done a hundred times before. Their feet moved together, hers backward, his forward, toes staying right against each other as they walked the five steps to the bed.

She thought she would ease onto it all seductively, but Trigger bit her bottom lip, then leaned down, picked her up, and tossed her unceremoniously on the bed like a caveman. A squeak escaped her, but she didn't have time to get angry at his surprise move because he was on her within a second. Between her legs, he rolled against her sex. Only his jeans and the thin material of her panties separated them, and she could easily feel his big, thick erection. A wave of possessiveness took her. *That's mine.*

What? Mine? Something was wrong with her. Or with him. He was making her feel…feel…well, he was making her feel. Why wasn't she running? Ooooooh, he was grinding against her now as he kissed her. Trigger gripped her wrists and slammed her hands against the bed above her head so now she was in a completely submissive position. No. No. No. This wasn't what she liked in the bedroom. She liked to be in charge. So why were there a million butterflies flapping around in her stomach right now? And why she was rocking her hips to meet him? Oh, she was in trouble. Deep, wide, humongous trouble. He smelled good. He'd been outside all that time doing God knows what, but he still smelled of hotboy deodorant, cologne, and something subtle. Something animalistic. Fur? Maybe he had a dog.

His stomach was flexing so hard against hers, and with every roll of his hips he was hitting her just right. She could finish like this so easily. Was that a thing? She hadn't dry humped since college.

"Ava," Trigger growled.

"Hmm?"

"Stop thinking. Just feel."

"I…I don't know how to do that."

He smiled against her lips and dragged his fingertips down her neck. "Feel good?"

"Yes," she answered breathily.

"And this?" he asked, grabbing her breast gently and massaging.

"Oh, yes," she whispered.

He trailed kisses down her jaw and clamped his teeth gently on her sensitive earlobe, then released her. "This?"

"Mmm hmmm."

Trigger eased back by a couple inches and slid his hand down the front of her panties. Without a second of hesitation, he pushed his finger into her and whispered, "That's a good girl," when she arched her back against the mattress and let off a soft groan.

Holy hell, Trigger was good. Really good. He was playing her body like a violin. He was hitting all the right pressure points, and now she was on fire with each stroke of his finger. And when he pushed a second finger into her, she gasped his name. She was lost. Completely lost. There were no other thoughts outside of whatever Trigger was doing to her. She closed her eyes and just...was.

He pushed into her harder, faster, and she rocked her hips to meet his touch. But right as she was on the verge of coming, right as she was raking her nails down his back and moaning in rhythm to the pace he was setting, right when her body was about to detonate around his fingers, he pulled out of her and jerked away. His movement was fast. Too fast. Her body was left cold, and he damn near blurred to the other side of the room.

"Shhhhit." He stood there panting, chest heaving with his breath, his neck and shoulders and face flushed, making the strange color of his eyes even brighter. He ran his hand through his hair, mussing it even more, and then he muttered, "I'm sorry," and walked out of the room. He didn't bother to close the door, but a few seconds later, she heard the forceful click of his own bedroom door.

And as she sat on that bed, leaned back on locked arms, her clothes all disheveled and her body feeling unsatisfied, the mysteries that surrounded Trigger Massey became even deeper. Before, she'd only wanted to do this job and leave as soon as possible, but now? A small curious part of her was sitting straight up and paying attention to that quiet man.

Maybe he didn't hate her after all.

Maybe he never had.

SIX

Sleep hadn't come easy for Trigger. In fact, sleep hadn't come at all. Fuck, if Colton found out he went after his sister, he would shoot him. Again. He had three bullet holes in his body from Colton trying to stop the bear from rampaging.

Colton was one of them good shots. Practiced. If this was the Wild West, Colton would've been one of those infamous gunslingers. He had the drive and eye for it, and thank God for small blessings, because three times Colton had redirected the bear's attention from wreaking havoc outside of the ranch.

He hadn't aimed to kill on those. If he found out Trigger had been fooling around with Ava last night, though? He'd put one through his heart and piss on his carcass.

And Trigger couldn't even blame him. He didn't have a sister, but he'd been super protective of Ava any time she dated a boy in high school. He had wanted to rip their innards out and hang them from a light pole. That wasn't sarcasm. He'd spent many a night lying awake, thinking of ways to kill the boys he imagined had their paws on his girl. Trigger frowned so deep his face hurt, and he pulled Harley to a stop. What the fuck. His girl? Ava wasn't his. She never was and she never would be. *Leave that girl alone.*

Harley blasted an impatient snort and dragged a front hoof through the snow. Beast. Trigger had asked him to stay still for three seconds and already the stallion was impatient. Well, he was gonna hate this next part.

Trigger sighed a froze breath and scanned the clearing. The frozen creek was giving him hell already this winter, and the cattle were thirsty. He still had a hundred head to keep alive until the auctions in the spring. That was his big payday. Maybe he could float the ranch another six months if he kept the herd safe. From himself.

He hated his life. Hated himself. He was full of

flaws and failing at everything. Dad had been so good at running this place, and when he'd gotten sick, where had Trigger been? Running a motorcycle club a few towns over, leaving all the work to Dad. Stubborn old mule didn't tell him how bad it was at the end, but Trigger should've seen it. He should've been here.

Harley stomped again and turned, clamped his teeth on Trigger's jeans and yanked his leg. It wasn't play. If Harley was more flexible, that asshole would've bit the tar out of his shin. Trigger had learned long ago to keep his legs back a few inches to avoid the bites.

He dismounted stiffly, as always happened the day after a Change when his body was screaming to stay in bed and recover. Yanking the reins, he pulled Harley over to an old felled tree and tied him off. With the other mounts, he could just wrap the reins once around a branch and they would stay put. With Harley though, he had to secure him better because the monster would run off the second he yanked free. Trigger had spent a whole lot of hours tracking down his runaway horse.

He bit the fingertip of his glove and jerked his

hand out of it, and with the glove hanging from his mouth, he pulled an ax from a tie on the saddle. And with the cattle bellowing around him, he went to work busting up the four inches of ice on top of the creek water, careful to check the mottled white and black bull's position regularly. He had an attitude to match Harley's, hated all people and animals other than his cows. If Trigger wasn't careful, he would get charged from behind and end up with cracked ribs thanks to the flying hooves of Deadfast Demon, a retired PBR bucking bull he'd gotten at a discount because he was a fence jumper with aggression problems.

Whatever it said about Trigger that he liked the mean animals the most, he didn't really care. This life out here required toughness. Submissive animals got eaten. By him. Deadfast would charge him and smash him in his bear face if he even tried to take a bite out of him. Trigger liked that shit.

The air was so cold it was burning his lungs, and as he broke through the layers of ice and exposed fresh water, the wind shifted. He inhaled twice just to make sure he wasn't imagining her, but nope. He had Ava's scent memorized from when they were kids.

Sure, she'd changed up her perfume, but her skin still smelled exactly the same.

And in an instant, the memories of how wet she'd felt as he slid his fingers into her washed through him. He had to get this under control. He had to get back to his ornery old self so she would stay away from him and do her job and leave. It wasn't for him that he wanted her gone. That was gonna feel like ripping his guts out, just like when she'd left here at eighteen. No, he needed her to leave for her own sake, her own safety. For her own chance at happiness. All he knew how to do was hurt people.

And Ava Dorset deserved so much better.

****

"I just don't understand why you won't let me see the inside," Ava murmured over the crunching of the snow under the horses' hooves.

"Because," Colton gritted out, "it's my cabin, and I don't want you in there. My territory. I don't have to explain. It ain't like you ever invited me to your fancy apartment in the city. So stop bellyaching about a lack of invitation into my den."

"Your den? Why do you talk so weird now?" She was staring at him, but all she got was his profile. He had been avoiding eye contact all morning. Great. Apparently, living with Trigger was making her brother weird, too.

"Lots of people call their houses 'dens.'"

"I've never heard it called that."

"Aaah! Ava! Are you gonna be on my case the entire time you are here? If so, I'm leaving. I'll go stay in town, and you can annoy Trigger instead. One day with you, and I'm maxed out."

"You just don't like anyone knowing your business, but I'm not just anyone, Colton. I'm your sister, and you're keeping me at arm's length. We have two weeks!" Frustrated, she said exactly what she wanted to. "Make me want to come back here again!"

Colton jerked a glance to her, but she gasped. His eyes were that strange color Trigger's had been in the cabin light. It was almost pure gold.

"What the fuck is wrong with your face?" she said so loud, the white filly named Queenie skittered a couple steps to the side, and she had to let her settle before she said at a less-psychotic volume, "What the fuck is wrong with your face?"

"I told you," he muttered, giving her his profile

again. He lowered his cowboy hat over his forehead. "Bear attack."

"That's not what I mean, and you know it. Are those contacts? Y'all can't afford more than beans for dinner but you're wearing colored contacts? Is it to get girls? I don't understand. You look fine the way you are." She huffed a breath and eased Queenie right beside his bay mount with four white socks. "Colton, you looked fine before. You know that, right? Before all the muscles and weird contacts."

"What are you getting at?" Colton asked in an irritated tone.

"I mean, just because your face is scarred up now, it doesn't mean you have to change other parts of yourself to take away from it. The scars look fine. I mean...they look badass. You survived a bear attack, and that story is written right on your face for everyone to see. Own it, big brother. Don't get a complex. Don't change other stuff about yourself to draw attention from the scars. You're fine just the way you are."

Colton ghosted her a glance, once, twice. On the third time, he offered her a curt nod and murmured, "What, did you major in? Psychoanalyst bullshit one-oh-one? Don't study me, *little sister*. I'm complicated, and you won't figure me out. That ain't a challenge either. I'm not broken, so don't try and fix me." With a fiery look, made a clicking sound behind his teeth while kicking his horse before trotting away toward a herd of milling, mooing cattle.

"Smells like cow poop," she complained under her breath as she watched him leave. "Specifically, it smells like bullshit, Colton."

"It ain't bullshit!" he called over his shoulder from much too far away to have been able to hear her. What the hell?

She was bundled up for the frigid morning weather, but still, she got chills on her forearms that prickled her skin uncomfortably. And then she saw him—Trigger. She'd been anxious to see him all morning while she'd gone through the stacks of paperwork on his finances that he left on the kitchen table for her to find this morning. She hadn't been able to focus, and her attention had drifted time and time again to the front window in hopes that Trigger was coming back for breakfast. When he didn't, she baked a can of buttermilk biscuits in the oven, buttered all of them, and packed them up in foil in hopes of keeping them semi-warm, then enlisted the help of Colton to find Trigger. He ran a ranch. For all she knew, he could be out all day working, and what if he didn't have food? Yeah, that had been her excuse to get to see him. Colton didn't even flinch when she asked him to help her saddle up Queenie, the ancient, scruffy white horse that looked just slow enough not to terrify Ava on her first ride in over a decade. She hadn't been in a saddle since she'd left Darby, Montana.

Colton seemed to be herding off a monstrous mottled white and black bull that had been dragging its hoof through the snow and inching closer to Trigger. But Colton cutting a path through the herd meant Ava had a clear view of the man who had surprised her so much last night.

He was slamming an ax into the ice over a little river. Each time he connected the blade to the frozen water, chips of ice exploded around him. In a smooth motion, he pulled the ax back and hurled it downward again. Trigger made it look easy, effortless, tireless, but she knew if she tried to lift that heavy ax, she would be worn out in ten swings and have blisters on her palms for days. God, he was sexy.

He wore jeans over work boots and an olive-green jacket with sheep wool lining around the collar. The cowboy hat he wore wasn't the same one as yesterday, this one more beige than cream, but it looked damn good on him. There was his black horse, Harley, pulling as hard as he could on his reins that were knotted to an old felled log. From the divots in the snow, the stallion had already dragged it about ten feet. She gave a private smile for his bad behavior and then guided Queenie to Trigger. He stopped and straightened his spine, but he didn't turn around as he growled out, "I'm working. What do you need?"

She was so taken back by his rudeness she couldn't find the words to answer. She'd thought they were past this. The whole fingering and fooling around and making out should've gotten them to a better place, not right back to square-freaking-one.

Trigger twisted, and his eyes were full of anger. "Ava, I have a million things on my plate right now. Say your needs and be on your way."

What was this hollow, aching sensation in her chest? Hurt? When was the last time she let a man hurt her? When Dad left. When he decided he didn't want to raise two teenage kids and would rather chase blackjack tables and horse betting. That was the last time. Until now.

She pursed her lips and blinked hard a few times. Damn him for making her feel weak, and double-damn him for making her eyes burn with these stupid tears. She wasn't a crier.

She tossed him the bag of foil-wrapped buttered biscuits, her appetite completely slaughtered now, and said, "I brought you breakfast. Enjoy your day. I'll ask finance questions later." And because she couldn't help herself, she added, "When you decide you can talk to me in a respectful manner, you pompous anal hair." And with her pink mitten-clad middle finger up in the air, she turned Queenie and made her way back through the milling cattle, because fuck him. And herself. She was so dumb for entertaining the idea of a crush on him.

Her cheeks heated like fire with embarrassment. She didn't do this. She didn't go out of her way for men. They rarely deserved the effort, and look what Trigger had done—proved her right once again. She wanted to hide under a rock.

"Fuck!" Trigger said so loud it echoed through the mountains.

Trigger appeared in front of her horse so fast she jumped. Queenie didn't, though. The old horse just came to a halt as Trigger yanked the reins out of Ava's hands. He offered her a gloved hand and glared up at her.

"What are you doing?" she asked.

"I'm offering an apology," he said low.

Not hearing any "I'm sorry," she crossed her arms over her thin black jacket and waited.

"Are you on your period?" he asked in a gravelly voice.

"What?" she yelled. Three cows right near them jumped and bolted away.

"You smell like blood, and plus you aren't normally this emotional. You look like you're about to cry, so…is it that time of your month? Your lady time? I can go to the store…" He cleared his throat and lifted his voice as he rolled his eyes heavenward. "I can go to the store and get you girl products and chocolate and ice cream and gossip magazines if you want."

Her lips made an embarrassing little popping sound as her mouth plopped open. "I cut my hand opening the fence to the barn this morning, and I didn't have a Band-Aid," she explained, pulling off her glove to show him the gash. It had made the palm of her mitten a darker pink. I'm not on my period. You just hurt my feelings. Apparently, I get more emotional around you, and I kind of hate it."

Trigger took off his hat and slid it back over his forehead in an agitated gesture. "Woman, you don't need to feel anything for me. It's a bad idea."

"Okay. Noted. I won't talk to you anymore. Can I have the reins back now?"

He bit his bottom lip and studied her for a few seconds too long to be polite. "No. You can eat breakfast with me."

"Oh, can I?" she said sarcastically. "How magnanimous of you. Polite decline."

"Get off the horse, Ava. That's as nice as I'm going to ask you."

"No."

His gold eyes narrowed to angry little slits. "Get. Down."

"Fuck. You."

With a terrifying sound in his throat, Trigger wrapped his arm around her waist and slid her off the saddle and onto the ground so fast her stomach dipped like she was on a roller coaster. She yelped as she landed with her sneakers deep in the snow.

Colton laughed from where he was now breaking up the ice for the cattle to drink. "She's gonna kill you in your sleep, man," he called unhelpfully. She was tempted about now.

Trigger was all worked up, his shoulders moving with his frozen breath, and his blazing eyes drifting from her eyes to her lips and back again. "I like you feisty," he growled.

She'd been ready to burn him with a retort, but that surprised her and drew her up short. "W-what?"

He leaned into her, mere inches from her ear as he gripped her waist. "It's so fucking hot that you fight everything. Makes me want to piss you off just to see your cheeks go red and your eyes go angry. You purse your lips when you're about to spew something poisonous at me, but it doesn't make me want to leave you alone, Ava. It makes me want to kiss you angry, just to see if I can get you to quit fighting."

"You're a monster," she whispered.

"You have no idea."

When he released her suddenly, she stumbled back a step. Her heart hammered against her ribcage as he straightened to his full height and looked down at her. "Ava Dorset, will you do me the honor of eating breakfast with me? First time I ever asked a girl nicely, so don't make me wait too long on an answer."

She crossed her arms over her chest again and looked from the black horse, who was still dragging the tree stump, to the bull that was inching closer to Trigger and rolling his angry eyes, to Colton, who was leaning on the ax and frowning at the back of Trigger's head, to the trio of pooping cows right near them, to Queenie, who was sleeping with one back hoof propped up, soft snores sounding from her, then finally back to Trigger. This was not the breakfast date she would've ever envisioned in a million years. But then again, sometimes "different" wasn't necessarily a bad thing.

"I could eat," she admitted.

Trigger nodded once and then turned and made his way toward the black horse, who promptly stopped dragging the log and bit at Trigger when he got close enough. The horse was as rude as his rider. Trigger didn't even seem to mind. In fact, he murmured something low and smiled as he pushed the horses head away, barely avoiding his teeth. Trigger pulled a thermos and a leather pouch from the saddle bags and then jerked his head toward a small grove of trees. She followed close behind, jogging to keep up with his long strides, until they reached a snow-covered bench that overlooked the creek in the shade of a towering pine.

As Trigger scooped snow off the bench seat, he told her something that shocked her to her bones. "Me and my dad built this when I was fifteen."

She studied the old cedar bench. Some of the boards had been replaced, and down one of the thick legs was what looked like splintered claw marks, like the ones on Colton's face.

"Don't worry, it's sturdy," he said, watching her face. There was still a layer of ice on the seat, but he removed his jacket and set it down, then gestured for her to take that spot.

"Won't you be cold?" she asked.

"Nah, I don't get cold easy, and besides, I've been working on busting up that ice for a while. I'm good. Go on."

"Okay," she said, shocked. Ava sat gingerly on the warm jacket and then wrapped it around her legs for good measure. Maybe he didn't get cold easy, but she sure did.

He handed her a couple of biscuits and then poured steaming coffee from the thermos into the lid before handing it to her. She didn't normally drink her coffee black, but she wasn't one to look a gift horse in the mouth either, so she murmured her thanks and took a sip. Not bad. He'd added vanilla to it, and it warmed her from the inside out.

After a few minutes of silent eating, Trigger draped his arm across the back of the bench and said, "You had questions."

"Oh," she said, feeling nervous. "Right. There is a big expense that I don't understand. You pay it out every month through your bank into an account that only shows up on this one payment on the fifteenth. Like clockwork for five years."

Trigger chewed a bite slowly and narrowed his eyes thoughtfully at Colton, who was tying Queenie to a shrub on the edge of the drinking herd of cattle.

"Five years ago, something awful happened."

"What?"

"Your brother got hurt. Bad hurt."

"The bear attack?"

77

Trigger dipped his chin to his chest once. "Right around that time, the neighboring ranch got hit by a bear, too. He slaughtered the entire herd and killed their livelihood. It's an older couple that runs that land, barely making it. The husband, Mr. Marks, he went after that bear, guns blazing, roughriding a horse he shouldn't have been on in the middle of the night. He fell and hurt his back. He had a family to feed, and I watched for a few months as his woman struggled to pull them up. And there came a time when I was watching Colton heal, watching what the bear had done to that family, and I had to help. Just...had to."

"Why you?"

"Why not me?"

"Do they know you're the one dropping money in their account?"

"No. That was the deal. They don't ask questions, and I keep them afloat."

"At the cost of your own ranch, Trigger. You understand that, right? You're losing this place. It's bad. It's really bad. You are in way over your head. Totally upside down on the mortgage, you owe everyone in town, and you aren't bringing in enough income to cover that family, much less yourself."

"I don't have a choice, Ava. I have to figure out a way to dig out."

"I crunched the numbers. This place is good. Good land, good access to the main road and to town. Someone could turn this into a tourist ranch, a dude ranch, or maybe someplace to do ATV excursions, something. Hell, the hunting around here is top-tier. Someone could come in and set up an outfitter. Get this place going again if they have the capital up front."

"Nah. I'm not selling. The bank would have to pry this place from my cold, dead hands."

"Why?"

"Because it was my dad's legacy." He looked over at her, and for the first time since she'd known Trigger Massey, there was pain in his eyes. "I let him down in life, Ava. Can't do that in death. Can't roll him over in his grave. He deserves better."

"He's dead, Trigger. You shouldn't let ghosts dictate your life."

"You did."

"What does that mean?"

"Isn't that what chased you away from here? Ain't

that why you ran? Your dad left. He ghosted on you, and you stayed as long as the state made you be in Colton's care, but the first chance you got, you bolted. I think sometimes our ghosts define us. Mine sure as hell does. I want to be half the man my dad was. Half the man, and I could die happy. If I let this place fold, or sell out, I have no shot at half-the-man in this lifetime."

Wow. Ava took another bite of a now-cold biscuit to stall her reaction. She'd never been sentimental about anything. Not anything materialistic and not places. She could pack up and move anywhere because a girl like her didn't get attached to anything. It had always been way out of reach. Her heart was cold and stubborn and didn't attach to warm things. Home was warmth. Trigger wasn't like what she'd thought. He wasn't cold. He attached just fine. His dead eyes when they were kids had been a mask. Trigger Massey was much deeper than she'd ever realized.

Now, she wanted to know everything about him. She wanted to figure him out. Wanted to unravel his many mysteries. "How did you let your dad down in life?"

"When you left, you missed a lot. Colton went wild. I went wild. The town was wild. Darby, and Charlos Heights, and Connor got overrun by MCs."

"MCs?"

"Motorcycle clubs. But not your normal ones. These settled in the small towns here because the law left them alone for the most part."

"Okay. And you joined one?"

"I ran one."

Ava choked on her biscuit and rushed to slurp down the remainder of her coffee. "You ran one," she repeated dumbly, trying to imagine him riding around on a motorcycle and doing...what exactly? "What do MCs do?"

"Illegal shit. I was president of Two Claws, and I was trying to keep the club's business legit, but the other clubs weren't doing the same and we caught flack for that. Devil Cats and Red Dead Mayhem fought for us to join each of their black-market stuff, and I tried to keep us neutral. But then they warred, and eventually I had to pick a side for us. It got people hurt. Got two of my guys killed." He grimaced like those words had tasted like poison.

"Was Colton in your MC?"

"He was my vice president."

"Oh, my God, how did I not know any of this?"

"Because you didn't answer his calls or come home, woman. Colton wasn't ever gonna email you this stuff."

"When did you two quit?"

Trigger huffed a humorless laugh. "You don't quit an MC, Ava. I tried. We got hit, and when two of my guys didn't make it, I dissolved the MC right after the funerals. Just...fucking demolished the entire club. Burned it to the ground, and then me and Colton bowed out and left no good leadership to help them rebuild. I couldn't stomach my club being pulled between the Devil Cats and Red Dead Mayhem anymore, so I killed the club."

"What happened to your members?"

"Some were okay with quitting after those funerals. Most joined the other two clubs. My dad passed away right after Colton was attacked, and my focus became this place. But I'm still paying for those MC days."

"How?"

"You saw my court fees? The dates?"

"Yeah. You found trouble with the law."

"Not until after I dissolved the club. I was never arrested while I was running it." He gave her the devil's smile. "I was never caught for anything." The smile faltered. "But dissolving the club pissed a lot of people off. I could've just handed it down to the ones who still wanted it up and running, but I didn't. I destroyed it from the inside out so that it could never exist again."

"So you get in fights over it?"

Trigger nodded once. "So I fight."

"Can't you stop?"

"I don't have it in me to back down, Ava. You should know that about me now. It won't ever change. If someone wants a fight, I have to give it to them. That's the way it is."

"Because of the type of man you are?"

"Because of the type of monster I am." He twitched his head hard, just like he'd done last night when he was talking to himself on the front porch. "What about you? I want to know about your life after you left. Was it happy? *Is* it happy?"

"I'm very fulfilled. I went to school, am working in the same field as the major I graduated with, I have an apartment, seven pet plants, and I cook. I have a routine, I work out, and everything about my life is in its exact right place. My financial planning business is taking off, and I'm right on the cusp of moving to a new level with bigger clients. Everything is moving in the exact direction I've worked for."

Trigger blinked slowly and straightened out one of his legs, the heel of his work boot digging into the snow. "You didn't answer my question."

"What question do you mean? Yes, I did."

"Are you happy?"

Well that took her back. Happy? It was routine and moving in a steady incline, so yes...right? "What do you mean happy?"

"Do you smile a lot? Do you laugh out loud, even when you're alone? Do you have friends you depend on for bad days and good days? Do you have a boyfriend? Do you hum to yourself or sing in the shower for no reason? Being fulfilled and being happy aren't necessarily the same thing."

Ava sighed and frowned. She'd never thought so deeply about this. "I guess I've been so focused on the outcome and where I wanted to get that I didn't really think about singing or smiling...or..." Well, now she was feeling definitely unhappy. "You know, you don't have to insult my life. It's a good one. I've worked hard for it."

"Oh, I have no doubt. You were always working harder than anyone around you. I knew you would go on to be successful. Is success what makes you happy?"

"Success is what makes me feel fulfilled. And now we're talking in circles, and I'm confused because until this conversation, I thought I was perfectly happy. Sometimes it's not very fun talking to you, Trigger."

"I get that a lot," he offered through a dead smile.

"You make me think, and maybe I don't want to think about this. Maybe I was happy thinking that I was happy, and now I'm questioning things, and it's not nice to do that to someone. Are *you* happy?"

"No. Never was and never will be. There are people in this world who are made to shoulder the troubles. They're made tougher because, from birth, their destiny isn't to experience joy. It's to exist, try to live a full life, and try to go out hurting as few people as they possibly can."

"That sounds like a very sad life. You could be happy, too, you know. Maybe find a girl who makes your heart beat a little faster and have, like, six wild little baby cowboy mini-Triggers running around here someday."

He chuckled and shook his head, gave his attention to the cattle drinking from the busted-up creek. "There is no girl for me, Ava. I've known that my whole life."

"What do you mean?"

"I wouldn't want to saddle one with who I am. No girl deserves that. Besides, I've had a woman make my heart beat faster before, and you know what happened?"

"What?"

He swallowed hard and then arced a serious, golden-eyed gaze to Ava. "She left." He rocked upward and dusted crumbs from his jeans. "I've got to get back to work. I need to drive the cattle back toward the barn and get some hay in them. Gotta million other things to do, too. Breakfast was...illuminating."

"Who left?" she asked, standing and handing him his jacket, nice and warm from her butt. "Do I know her?"

"You know her very well." He tipped his hat and

gave her a crooked smile. "Ma'am. I sure thank you for breakfast."

As he walked away, a thought hit her like a lightning strike. Before she could change her mind, she called, "Was it me? Did I make your heart beat faster? Was I the one who left?"

He didn't answer.

"Trigger! What would make you happy?"

He slowed and turned, walked backward a few paces as he said, "Saving my dad's legacy." With a sad smile, he turned back around and made his way to the black horse.

It was her. She knew it in her bones. She'd been so wrong about Trigger when they were kids. He'd kept himself rude to her for reasons she didn't understand. He'd kept her at arm's length...but why?

Saving his dad's legacy...

The stubborn bits of her...and the caring ones...they vowed in this moment to try to help him find happiness.

She had two weeks, and she didn't know *how* she would save this place.

Only that she would.

SEVEN

Ava read over the top four items of the to-do list with a frown.

Grocery shopping
Snow boots and warmer jacket
Settle the general store bill
Settle the bar tab at the GutShot

The last two were confusing. She'd called both of them earlier and been given the runaround for two-hundred-dollar debts. They'd both sent Trigger to collections multiple times, but when she'd tried to pay over the phone as a surprise for him, both owners had refused to settle the tab. So okay, she was going to have to handle this face-to-face. She was tough when she wanted to be. A ball-buster, according to the B's in her office. Ben, Bernie, and Brad liked to rag on her for being too masculine when she was in a get-shit-done mode, but that's what a woman had to be in the business world, right? A spit-fire. A ball-buster. A man-eater. If a man acted like that, it was business as usual, but a woman had to take control, take no shit, and also deal with the names associated with being firm and outspoken.

She yanked the truck keys off the hook near the door and clamped her teeth over the keyring as she struggled into her thin jacket and mittens, then her pink winter hat with the fluffy snowball on the top. The door was a strange one. It looked like it was made of rusted iron. It was at least eight inches thick and didn't match the rustic décor. It looked too industrial to go with the cabin. Just as she reached for the handle, that heavy door swung open. She gasped as she came face-to-face with Trigger. He wore snow-dusted jeans and the same blue plaid shirt he'd worn yesterday before he'd ended up butt-naked in a blizzard.

His startled face probably matched hers, and they

just stood there, staring at each other. His shoulders had snow on them, and the beige cowboy hat was pulled low over his eyes. It didn't cover the striking color, though. She didn't remember his eyes like this when they were kids, but then again, he'd never looked at her much. Well...not that she'd known of.

"Your hat's cute," he rumbled in a gritty voice.

"It is?"

One corner of his lips turned up in a breathtaking crooked smile that left her stunned. He reached up and ruffled the yarn snowball on top. "Pink looks pretty on you. Matches your cheeks. Rosy."

"Pink and black is my favorite color combination," she murmured lamely.

The other corner lifted now and she couldn't pull her attention from his lips if she tried. "Mine's brown and green."

"That's boring," she teased.

When the smile dipped, she became desperate to fix it. "Green and brown because those are the colors around your ranch?"

Trigger shook his head. "I'm colorblind. It's about all I see."

"Oh." She straightened her hat and fidgeted with

the keys. "Have you always been colorblind?"

"Yep. Just like my dad. And my grandpa. And his grandpa. All the men in my family are."

"What about the girls?"

"Well, girls don't get this kind of colorblindness, and even if they did, my family doesn't make baby girls. Only boys."

"Well, maybe you'll be the exception to the rule someday," she chirped optimistically.

He chuckled darkly. "I don't think so. I can only make boys, and besides all that, I ain't made to parent a kid. Someday you'll come back here, older, married, wanting to spend the holidays where you grew up, spend them with your brother." His voice dipped low and soft, and his gaze dropped to the floorboards. "You'll be beautiful still. Hair all done up, eyes still the same cornflower blue. Maybe wearing glasses. Laugh lines deeper. You'll be surrounded by noise. Surrounded by your grown babies and their babies and your smile will still be just as pretty. And me? I'll be just like I am now. In this place if I'm really lucky. Alone, a gnarled old bachelor, just happy I get that moment to watch you and where you ended up, surrounded by the good stuff. By the grit that makes a life worth livin'." His eyes were haunted as he lifted that steady gaze to hers. "Do that someday, okay? Come back for Colton. Bring him family. Come back and let me see where you ended up."

"Okay," she murmured, confused on why he seemed so sad.

He gave her a phantom of a smile, pushed past her, and then strode with echoing bootsteps toward the hallway.

"Hey, Trigger?" she asked.

"Yeah?"

She shuffled her feet, stalling, because she was scared of him rejecting her when he had her heart pounding like this. "Do you want to go into town with me?"

"For what?" he asked, his chin jerking a little.

"I have a to-do list, and also I'm hungry for anything other than beans."

"You wanna do dinner?"

She grinned slyly. "Are you asking?"

Trigger turned slowly, squared up to her. He waited a few seconds, studying her face, so she stayed patient, because men like Trigger Massey required quiet persistence.

"Ava Dorset. Do you want to eat dinner with me?" he asked at last.

"Depends," she said cheekily. "What kind of food are you offering?"

His grin stretched his face and transformed him into something beautiful, if that term could be applied to a beast of a man like him. "Barbeque."

Of course he'd offered her meat. She would never admit it out loud, but he'd just listed the food of her heart. She mirrored his smile and said softly, "Deal."

"I'll drive then. You probably don't even remember how to drive on ice anymore, City Slicker."

She wanted to be offended, but his little smirk made her want to play. "We could always ride that horrid horse of yours into town."

Trigger snorted. "Harley would scrape you off at the first tree. He doesn't like girls." Trigger frowned. "Or boys, children, snakes, frogs, lightning bugs, tree branches, grass, dirt, bumble bees, Colton especially, other horses, being tied to anything, the type of grain I feed him, or his life in general. He's a bit of an asshole."

Ava giggled. "But the way you called him an asshole sounded like a term of endearment. You love that monster."

"I love nothing."

"Oh, because you're heartless?" she asked, zipping up her jacket crisply.

"That's right. There's only gristle in my chest cavity." He zipped up his own jacket with the wool lining at the collar. It fit him well, and he cut a fine V-shaped figure, his muscular arms pressing against the sleeves. He'd felt really good last night when he'd put just the right amount of pressure on her body with those strong arms.

"You thinkin' dirty thoughts?"

"No!"

His black eyebrows arched up as he laughed. "Bullshit. A, you're thinking really loud. B, it's written all over your face. And C, I can practically smell your pheromones. That was fun last night, but it can't happen again. I was wrong to come at you needy like that. I was just—"

"Cold from being randomly naked in a blizzard?"

Trig gave an eyeroll and gestured to the door. "Let's go warm that truck up. He's old, and it takes a few minutes."

"That's what she said," Ava muttered.

"Great, you're a pervert now. This next two weeks should be fun."

"For me. I get to watch you try and resist me in my holey, saggy pajamas and the retainer I have to wear at night to keep my two front teeth straight. And those glasses you mentioned earlier? Already have 'em. I'm already aging. Can you see my deep laugh lines?" She pointed to the corner of her eye and tried to keep a straight face while she gave him a questioning glance.

"Twenty-eight isn't old, you little psychopath. You're still a spring chicken. Me, however, I've got a bum trick knee, and even if I had no instincts for weather at all, I could tell a storm's coming just from my aching leg. That's old man shit right there."

He'd never talked so easy, and Ava had trouble taking her eyes from his mouth as he talked. Even the way he formed words was unfamiliar and interesting. He had a scar down one side, a small one, mostly hidden by his dark, trimmed beard.

"What happened to your lip?"

"Fighting," he answered without a single millisecond of hesitation. Trig pushed open the door for her and then waited until she made her way outside before he followed.

"That's a serious door." Ava pointed to the iron barrier. The rust color matched the metal numbers nailed onto a plaque right above an old beer bottle opener someone had nailed beside the old porch swing. There were long cuts in the wood that were splintered in places. Those numbers made her smile though. One zero, one zero. She'd always loved numbers that repeated themselves.

"I'll tell you something silly."

"Serious Ava with a silly story? All right, let's hear it. I'm mentally prepared."

She flicked her pink mitten clad fingertips at the 1010. "Sometimes I make wishes on numbers that repeat."

"Superstitious? I wouldn't have called that."

"Not really superstitious. I just like the idea that you can make a wish and something good happens, just because you think positively about it. Just because you want it real bad."

Trig had gone completely still and serious. "What would you wish for right now? Right this minute?"

Lifting her chin high, she rested her pointer finger on the number and closed her eyes. *I wish I could save this place.*

When she opened her eyes, Trig was watching her with an unreadable expression. And after a few seconds, he touched the 1010 and closed his eyes and went still. And when he opened his eyes, they were a little darker, a little less wild.

She would bet her bones they had just made the same wish. She wouldn't admit it because he wouldn't understand the reasons she was getting invested in saving this place. Hell, she didn't understand it herself. There was something about Trig. Something about the way he was now as a man. Something about how he'd always seemed aloof when they were kids, but he'd paid more attention to her than she'd realized.

She had a feeling she had been wrong about a lot.

He held out his hand, and she dropped the keys onto the scuffed-up material of his glove. Bustling to keep up, she followed his long strides through the snow and around to the back of the cabin. There was a detached garage made of logs that matched the home. When he yanked open the door, she gasped as she entered. There were three Harley Davidson motorcycles and an old Ford truck in two-tone brown. It looked old as dirt, but it was clean and had new tires. She followed him to the truck, and as she slid onto the clean, maroon, leather bench seat, Trig turned the engine and it blared right to life.

"I fixed this up. Bought it for a thousand dollars. Dumped two grand into it, and I'll keep running it into the ground until I can't save it anymore." Trig blasted the heat, which was frigid air, currently, and pointed the vents at her. "Maybe when you come back someday, I'll still be driving the same truck."

"You have it in your head that you'll be stagnant forever."

"Is that a bad thing?"

"No. Not necessarily. If it's what you want. If it's what makes you happy and keeps your soul steady."

"My soul steady," he repeated low. "I like that."

"Those Harleys. How much are they worth?"

"Not for sale."

Her breath froze in front of her face with the put-upon sigh she offered him. "Trig, you're going to have to make some sacrifices for this place."

He huffed a single laugh. "I've sacrificed plenty."

"How much," she gritted out as he pulled the Ford out of the garage.

A strange sound emanated from his chest. It sounded downright feral, and chills rippled up her forearms. "Fifteen each for the older ones. The newer one is mine. Giving it up would mean giving up a piece of me. It would be giving up my ability to have a shit day and rip out of here on the bike and just get lost for a while."

"That's what it's like? An escape?"

"Have you never been on a Harley before?"

"Never. I'm a safe, well-behaved good girl with a firm belief in seatbelts."

When Trigger made a snoring noise, like she was boring, she whacked him on the arm. "One of us is going to survive to old age, and one of us is going to make questionable decisions that jeopardize his safety and—"

"As soon as this snow clears, I'm taking you out on a ride."

"What? No. Seat belts. Were you not just listening to my concerns?"

"Woman, stop," he demanded, casting her a frown. "What's the point of living until old age if you forget to live on your way there?"

Well that drew her up. She wanted to be witty

and smart and come up with some epic retort that made him bow down to her impeccable style of arguing, but she just sat there with her mouth hanging open. Again. "I thought you were a dumb jock."

"What?" he asked, resting one arm over the wheel and one on the edge of his window as he guided them down the snowy driveway that led to the main road.

"You played all the sports and never talked. You were always rude to me, but I saw you pay attention to other girls. I assumed you charmed them with your face, not your intelligence."

"God, you're a pill." But the smile that tugged at the corner of his mouth said he didn't mind her pill-like qualities. "I was good at sports, but I also made good grades. Does that turn you on, Nerd?"

"I was not a nerd! I skipped class twice. Mr. Redding's science class. I hid in the bathroom, and once I smoked a cigarette with Barbie MacDonald."

"She was bad," he drawled with a chuckle.

"She was the biggest rebel I knew! I looked up to her! She offered me a smoke in the bathroom, and I felt like a badass until I coughed a lot and she yanked the cigarette out of my hand and stomped off."

"In those combat boots of hers?"

"Yep, she always wore them. I tried to buy a pair on clearance once, but I couldn't pull them off, so I returned them. Barbie was so cool."

"Barbie still lives here and probably wears the same shoes. She has matured zero percent while you..."

Ava pulled her legs up crisscross-applesauce to conserve heat. "While I what?"

"You grew into a woman."

The way he said "woman" gave her the strangest fluttering sensation deep in her stomach.

Trigger continued, "The minute you start looking at someone else and thinking they have their shit together...you fail yourself. The minute you look at someone else and wish for their life? You fail yourself. You're doing just fine, and you never needed to be anyone but you. You were always the one to look up to. You just didn't see it."

"Did you? See it?"

"What's on the to-do list?"

"Trigger! You've been inside of me. You owe me answers."

"My fingers have been inside you, not my dick."

"There's a difference? I mean, besides the fact that your dick is the size of a damn mutant eggplant—"

"Jesus, Ava," he muttered with a scrunched-up face. "Don't use the word mutant when you talk about a man's cock."

"Oh, my God, you just said 'cock.' Like in a romance novel."

Trig snickered and leaned his head back on the rest, eyes on the snowy road. "I saw you just fine back then."

"Why were you so rude to me all the time?"

"I wasn't rude. I was just…safe."

The air coming out of the vents was finally warming up, so she held her fingers in front of it. "Explain safe."

"I paid attention to the girls who didn't matter."

Ava's heart rate picked up double-time, and she kept her attention carefully on the pink material of her mittens. "Did I matter?"

"Yeah. And that's all you get today because I only put two fingers in you. If it was my mutant cock, you could have all the answers you want."

"You don't play fair."

"Never said I did."

When she let off a growl, he laughed. "Did you just growl at me? That was the least terrifying thing I've ever heard."

"You talk a lot. It surprises me," she said suddenly. "You used to be so quiet. I would forget what your voice sounded like some weeks."

"I'm quiet around strangers. That whole school was full of people who felt risky."

"Did I feel risky?"

"More than anyone else there."

"Did you have a crush on me, Trigger Massey?"

"Nah, I didn't get crushes. Heartless, remember? Besides, you were dating around."

"Dating around with two boys, not sleeping with, so don't even hint that I was a ho."

"Remember that guy you dated freshmen year?"

A sliver of discomfort snaked its way through her middle. "I don't want to talk about this."

"Well, we need to because I got suspended for you."

"What?" she yelped.

"Eddie Young was bragging about getting to second base with you in the locker room. I was a senior. Colton was in there, too. We were trying to keep our cool, but your brother was pissed, and I was pissed, and Eddie was making you sound easy to everyone in the locker room. I knew the whole school would be talking about it by lunch time. *Knew it.* You were gonna get bad hurt by the things people said, so…"

"So, what?"

"So, I beat the shit out of him. In front of everyone. I gave them something else to talk about."

"That's why you got suspended? You didn't get to walk the stage for graduation!"

"So?"

She just stared at his profile. Things were sooo different from what she'd thought. All these years, she'd hated him, misunderstood him, been confused by him. She'd been uncomfortable just thinking about him, and he'd secretly been her champion. And he hadn't even done it for credit. He'd hid it, taken his punishment quietly. Ava pulled her mitten off and chewed on the edge of her thumbnail. She gave her attention to the piney woods that blurred by. "If you could go back, would you do it just the same?"

"No."

"What would you have done differently?" she asked.

"Homecoming dance," he said without hesitation. "I was graduating that year, was thinking about leaving for college, and you were nice. You tried to be. You were with your friends at the dance, and I was sitting with Colton on the other side of the gym on the bleachers. The DJ announced it was ladies' choice on the next song."

"I remember this," she murmured, the picture of the gym covered in rainbow balloons and colorful lights on the floor and the music up so loud the bass rattled her chest.

"I watched you the whole night," Trig continued. "When you looked over at me and started walking across the dance floor, I knew I was gonna have to say no. There was this part of me that wanted you to turn around. Get distracted and dance with someone else. But then there was a bigger part of me that wanted you to ask me, just so I could keep that moment."

"Keep it?"

"Yeah, for a memory."

"I asked you, and you told me to go dance with

Eddie instead. I was hurt because he'd been spreading rumors about me, then you'd rejected me and pushed me toward someone who hurt me."

"I told you to dance with Eddie because I knew he wasn't there that night. I'd gone to his house and told him if he ruined your night, I'd do a locker room repeat on his face. Plus, it got it out of your head to pay attention to me."

"You liked me. I know because you terrorized a boy who was mean to me. If you didn't like me, you wouldn't have cared. You wouldn't have put in that effort. That boy is probably traumatized because of you."

Trigger eased the old Ford onto Main Street, the wheels sliding slightly on the icy surface. "I hope he is. You should know I don't carry guilt about that kind of stuff. You should see me for what I am. I don't feel bad for fighting. I don't have that chip that tells me to look back at fights and regret them. A fight comes, I take care of it, and then I move to the next one."

"You're warning me you are dangerous."

"Very."

"I saw how many times you've been arrested in your paperwork. All the bail money you had to pay

Colton back for. You're an outlaw."

Trig shrugged his shoulder. "That word doesn't bother me. The law works differently for people like me."

"People like you?"

"Men with animals inside of them."

She frowned so deep her forehead hurt. "What do you mean?"

"There is something inside of me that is more instinct than logic. It was like that when I was born, and it'll be like that until the day I draw my last breath. I'm not like you. I feel less and react more. And when I snap, whoever sets me off needs to stay the fuck out of my way."

"Are you telling me I'm in danger?"

He huffed a small laugh and shook his head. "I couldn't hurt you if I tried. I don't hurt women, but especially you. You're so safe, it's ridiculous. No one will ever mess with you while you're around me, or they'll be swallowing their teeth."

More chills blasted up the back of her neck. Part of her was horrified by his admissions, but part of her, in this moment, truly did feel safe. Had she felt that before? Had she ever felt like someone would truly have her back? Even in bars, she never looked to her friends to get her out of a rough situation with a pushy guy. She didn't look to anyone, because after Dad left, she didn't trust anyone. Not Colton, not any friends...only herself. But with Trigger? She had this soul-deep feeling that he was telling the truth, and if she needed someone at her back, he would already be there. Quietly watching her and defending her like he'd done in locker rooms and at homecoming dances.

Trigger was special. He was getting her attention like no man ever had. He was calling to parts of her she hadn't known existed, and now it felt like he was changing her.

She should run...right? She had her whole life together, every aspect, and was on a steady incline to a truly successful life, but here was this man telling her exactly how dangerous he could be, guiltlessly, and she was finding herself scooting closer to him.

Trouble. Trig was trouble. She was a good girl, and he was a bad boy, and what good would it do her to get a crush on a man like that? He had a rap sheet, a wild streak, and he was unapologetic for both.

His chronic wildness was why he'd been rude.

Why he'd ignored her when they were kids. Trig wasn't selfish by nature. He knew his path, knew himself, knew he was missing that rule-minding chip, and he'd already commented on not being surprised at her success. He'd seen their futures for exactly what they would be, and he'd protected her, once again, in his own way. Protected her from him.

She could see it all now. If he'd given in and talked to her, she would have gotten addicted to him. Would have fallen in love with him. Where would she be now? In this small town still? A baby on her hip and two more on her ankles, trying to salvage a ranch that was on its last leg and watching Trig struggle under the weight of it. Where would her career be? Her livelihood?

He'd made sure she had the chance to get the life she wanted.

Trigger Massey might be a bad boy, but he was a very good man to her.

EIGHT

Trigger watched her move. He couldn't help himself. She was poetry as she walked down each aisle with her clumsy, human grace. He noticed everything. The arch of her hand as she reached for an apple. The curve of her lips as she teased him for not eating enough vegetables. The clear, crystal blue in her eyes as time and time again she looked over her shoulder at him. She was magic. Ava had the power to slow time. Every moment dragged onto three, and thank God for small blessings, because this woman would be out of his life in two weeks. And this two weeks would have to last him a lifetime.

He was pushing the cart, couldn't help it. He wanted to do little things to make her life easier. He'd

FOR THE LOVE OF AN OUTLAW

done it when they were kids, but she'd just never noticed. Now he thought maybe she did. Now he thought maybe she was paying attention. Now he thought maybe she saw him more clearly.

"You're such a quiet man with other people," Ava murmured as she dropped a bag of spaghetti pasta into the cart. "Not as quiet as when we were kids, but you're watchful."

A private smile curved his lips because, yep, he'd been right. She was paying attention.

He admitted, "I like it better when you talk."

"I talk a lot."

"It's perfect. You talk and take all the attention, and I'll be your quiet bodyguard."

She giggled. "What would I need a bodyguard for? No one messes with me." She tossed him a cheeky grin over her shoulder. "I'm too tough, and people don't even try."

"Mmm," he murmured noncommittally. Probably best because he'd pop their fuckin' heads from their bodies if they tried.

He smelled him before he saw him. The scent of fur was as familiar to him as anything. Kurt Engle rounded the corner with an armload of beer and a bag of pork rinds in the other hand. "Holy shit," he said when he saw Trigger. "Look what the cat dragged in." His smile got even brighter when his attention landed on Ava, who was checking the nutrition facts on a bag of pretzels.

Kurt approached her slow. "Hello, New Girl. Ain't seen you around here before."

Ava lifted her attention to the six-foot, black-haired, cat-eyed giant.

"I'm from here," she said. "Ava Dorset." She stuck her hand out for a shake.

Kurt looked at Trigger like he'd just seen a unicorn, laughed, and then bit the bag of pork rinds to shake her hand. "Whoo!" he said, shaking his hand out. "Firm handshake, New Girl. I bet you're dangerous with a grip like that." He gave Trigger a wink, and Trigger straightened up from where he'd been leaning on the cart.

"She's got plenty to do with that grip already. Fuck off, Kurt."

"Geez, territorial much? Is she yours?"

Ava was frowning up at Trigger, but she didn't understand the dynamics here.

"She's her own. She's only here for a visit."

"So not yours," Kurt said with a slight frown.

Trigger swallowed the growl that clogged his throat. "She's mine while she's here." The scent of fur intensified and, fuck it all, apparently the whole damn clan was here.

As the three other cougars of the Darby Clan flooded into the aisle, Trigger pulled Ava behind him and slid a glance to the open end of the aisle to check an escape. The alpha, Chase, was leaned against the end shelf with a dead smile plastered to his face. His right eye was still messed up from when Trigger beat the shit out of him two weeks ago. Shifters healed a little faster than humans, but it looked like Chase had needed surgery if the stitches and bruising were anything to go by.

"Not lookin' for trouble," Trigger grumbled.

"You never are," Chase said, pushing off the shelf and meandering closer. "Trigger, Trigger with the heart of gold and that moral compass that just fucks up everyone's plans. You gotta new girl, Hairpin?" Turning to Ava, he said, "This is a dangerous game. We call that one Hairpin Trigger. That one has a temper." His nostrils flared as he scented the air, and Trigger new just what he was looking for. Right now, that oversensitive nose of his was telling the alpha that Ava was human. Fragile. Breakable. "May want to rethink your life decisions, Little Lady," he murmured, lifting a strand of her shoulder-length hair as he passed.

Ava flinched back and slapped his hand, and Trigger's reaction was immediate. He grabbed Chase by the back of the neck, and when his clan surged forward, he shoved the alpha into them. "I said I ain't looking for trouble. Not that I won't go to fuckin' war again if you push me, Kitty. Touch her again, and I'll even up the stitches on the other side."

"Okay, okay," Chase said, hands up in surrender as he looked up at a security camera on the ceiling. Wily old cat always knew where those were. He was real practiced at getting Trigger into trouble.

"I think you all should walk away," Ava said with a surprising amount of steel in her voice. She was looking Chase dead in the eye, too, spine straight, chin up, not backing down an inch. Sexy, sexy Ava.

Trigger couldn't help the feral smile that stretched his cheeks. "You heard her. We got pretzels to buy, boys."

"And also mini bottles of wine because the beer

you and Colton drink is gross."

Trigger snorted and corrected himself. "And cheap wine for the lady."

Ava dismissed them. "You boys have a nice night."

And she didn't give those cougars her back once as they filtered out of the aisle one by one, until only Kurt was left.

"It was good to see you again, Hairpin," he said softly.

"Kurt!" Chase yelled.

Kurt lowered his head and followed the Darby Clan.

"Who was that?" Ava asked, turning to face him.

Trigger waited until the scent of the big cats had faded before he inhaled deeply, gave one last glance to the security camera, and pulled her against his chest. Why he did that, he didn't have a damn clue. This really was dangerous territory. She was doing something shocking to his bear. She was settling the monster in his middle.

Slowly, she slid her arms around his waist and held on tight, the bag of pretzels crinkling in her fist.

It was one of those moments...the ones that changed a man from the bones out. She'd stood tall beside him and glared those cats down, trusted him to keep her safe, and then went soft against him in the next minute. He'd done this alone for so long. He even hid the grit from Colton when he could, but standing here in the middle of a grocery store, his heart pounding against the cheek of a woman he'd thought about all these years, he didn't really want to do this alone anymore. He wanted purpose, and not just to save the ranch. He wanted someone to push him to be better. He wanted a girl to save the ranch for. And not just any girl. It had always been Ava.

He dropped his lips to the top of her head and let them linger there as he inhaled her scent. Against her soft tresses, he murmured, "They aren't men."

It was the biggest, scariest admission of his life. Dad had ingrained it in him to hide what he was—always.

"What are they?" she asked.

"Animals."

"Oh. Who was the nice one?"

The way she asked the question so quickly, with no reaction to his admission, said she didn't really understand what he'd told her. Trigger sighed. "That's Kurt Engle. He used to run with me, and now he runs with Chase and his boys. He was a friend once. Now he's not."

Ava ran her fingers gently up and down his back, her nails making zipping sounds against his jacket. "That's sad."

"What is?"

"The loss of a friendship."

"Nah, that's life. People come and go. Most of them are only in your life to get you somewhere. And what I mean by that is they are supposed to teach you lessons, and then you grow or learn something hard and you don't make those mistakes again. And if you're lucky, you have a handful of people who stick around because they're supposed to. Those are the ones it's sad to lose. Kurt was never one of those."

"Colton is?"

Smart, smart girl caught on to what he was saying. "Yeah, like Colton. It didn't hurt when Kurt flipped sides. If Colton had though, it would be one of those big life lessons."

"Like the one I learned when my dad left?"

"What do you mean?" Trigger asked.

"If Colton left you, you would turn bitter and cold and you would never let anyone else in."

"Yes. That. He's been in my life too long to let him go easy. Is that what happened to you when your dad left?"

She nodded, but backed away from talking about old scars. With a bright smile, she said, "You two have a bromance. Which is weird to say because he's my brother. Do you know he won't let me in his cabin?"

Trigger snorted. "That's nothing personal."

"It sure feels personal."

God, her nails running up and down his spine were getting him half hard already. Usually he kept everything to himself, but he wanted to reward her for settling him. "He's got a pet squirrel he named Genie. He calls it his wishing squirrel. She's a little tyrant who runs his whole damn life, and she doesn't like new people in her territory."

Ava had frozen against him, her fingertips pausing right in the middle of his back. "Colton has a squirrel?"

"Yep." His best friend got stranger with age.

A little old lady puttered by and slapped Trigger on the ass as she pushed her cart past them. He flinched and swallowed a curse, rolled his eyes heavenward, and prayed for patience.

Ava turned and stared, open mouthed, at Martha Lane, the town eighty-year-old boy-chaser and frequent slapper-of-asses.

He cleared his throat and released Ava. "On that note, I'm feeling nice and violated and ready to blow this popsicle stand."

Ava whispered, "Martha's still got it."

He snorted and watched Martha waggle her thick gray eyebrows as she scooped an entire armload of Fritos into her cart.

And damn it all, he was trying not to smile to encourage the woman, but Ava let off the cutest peel of giggles he'd ever heard in his life and, yeah, his life was really fuckin' weird. Between the clan, Colton's wishing squirrel, and the molestation by a hundred-pound woman with silver bouffant hair who was now licking her lips at him, there wasn't much normal about his current existence. And thank God, Ava had a good sense of humor about it, because he needed this. He needed to hear her laugh grow and his laugh get bigger in his belly instead of his usual reaction to an almost-fight, which was a Change in the woods and hunting something the damn predator inside of him required. He needed blood either way, fighting or hunting. But right now? Trigger felt fine, other than the sting of Martha's little handprint on his left buttcheek.

"Wine and go," he murmured.

"Fine, but I feel left out," Ava said, giving him this fucking adorable, little wicked look.

"How so?"

"You got a spanking, but I didn't."

Most of his body froze. His dick however, did not. It pressed against the front seam of his jeans as he imagined Ava riding his cock and him slapping her soft skin right on her perfect, round left cheek. And the monster in him wanted to mark her. Especially if she liked that, which from the way she held his gaze with challenge flashing in her eyes, Ava sure did like it. Fuck, she was perfect.

"It's not a good idea to tease a man like me about that stuff, Ava. I'll have a perfect handprint on your ass before you leave this store if you test me enough." Hell, he would have her against the shelf of chips if she tested him enough, and damn the camera above them. He'd give them a show, have her screaming his name. Ever since he'd felt how wet she got for him last night, felt inside of her body, he couldn't stop imagining his dick inside her. Tough Ava. Strong woman who never let anyone get too close. Runner. Beauty. Challenge. He'd never wanted to possess a person as much as Ava. It had always been like that. She didn't roll over easy. She didn't give in. She lived her life exactly how she wanted, and she didn't let anyone stand in the way of what she wanted. This woman didn't tiptoe through life. She stomped through it and didn't care about the noise she made.

Perfect personality to tame a beast like him.

Trigger shook his head hard. That wasn't right. That was his animal putting thoughts in his head. *Stop it, Bear.* He was getting confused. Two weeks, and she needed to go. Two. Weeks. Thirteen more days and then...nothing.

Ava was frowning up at him like he'd lost his mind. "I've got some business up at customer service. Can you grab me one of those four packs of the mini bottles of cheap rosé?"

"Why don't I just get you a bottle? It's cheaper."

But she was already marching from the aisle, leaving him good and confused. What the hell had just happened? They were having a good moment, and then bam. She was gone. Martha flicked her tongue out at him and, fuck this, he was going to follow Ava. Just to make sure she was safe. Yep. Just to make sure the cougars didn't mess with her.

Because he had big instincts now, ones he hadn't felt since she'd lived in town. Since he was a teenager. He'd been protective of his motorcycle club, but not like this. There was this unsettled feeling inside of him, and all his senses blared when she left his sight. What if she tripped or whacked an endcap with her hand and cut herself? Or rolled an ankle or got flu germs from the cart or...? Oh, dear God, he was losing his mind.

Ava would run the second he tried to suffocate her with attention like this.

Oh, who the hell was he kidding?

Ava was going to run anyway.

NINE

"I just don't understand why you won't let me pay his bill," she said for the third time.

The woman in customer service, Charlotte, her nametag read, was a sour-faced old bitty with what looked to be permanent frown lines on either side of her mouth and who wore about a gallon too much perfume. "Because it's Trigger Massey," she answered, also for the third time.

Ava plastered a smile on her face, though it probably looked more like a frown, and then clutched her purse strap in a strangle hold to control herself from choking this unhelpful heifer. "Charlotte. That's a lovely name, by the way. It's a two-hundred-dollar bill, which started out as twenty-three dollars and

eighteen cents for one grocery bill on a lean month.
You sent him to collections before the billing cycle
was even through, and you've charged him interest
for the past three months. I can't believe you would
make it this difficult on purpose. He's trying to do the
right thing and pay his debt, so surely you wouldn't
keep someone from doing that on purpose. Would
you? Do you mean I can't pay it because I'm not
Trigger? He needs to pay it? Because I can go grab
him, and we can take care of this right now."

Charlotte popped a big pink bubble with her gum
and chewed loudly three times before she said in a
bored voice, "You better not fuckin' bring him up
here, lady. Hairpin Trigger ain't welcome at customer
service."

"Why not?" Ava said too loudly, completely
irritated now.

Charlotte gave her an empty smile. *Smack. Smack.
Smack* went her gum. "Because he don't pay his
debts."

Ava pursed her lips against a scream. "Well, all
right then, I can see you've been as helpful as you can
possibly be, Charlotte," Ava said, connecting a call on
her phone.

A flicker of worry drifted across Charlotte's face. "What are you doing?"

Ava leaned on the counter, and when Ben picked up at her office, she gave him the code phrase. "Hello, this is Ava Dorset with Dorset Financial Planning. I'm having trouble paying a bill to keep a client from another round of collections."

"Damn, again?" Ben asked. "Okay, bla, bla, bla, give her the 'serve the paperwork' spiel now."

"Oh, you can have the paperwork drawn up today? That's fantastic. When can I expect them to be served?"

"List the place," Ben said in a bored voice, the sound of his mouse clicking in the background.

"Remmy's Grocer, Darby, Montana—"

"That's enough," Charlotte exclaimed, reaching for the phone.

Ava jerked away and gave her a narrow-eyed warning look. "It's right off Main Street—"

"Fine! Just pay his bill and be done."

"Great," she muttered. "She seems to be working with me again for now," she said to Ben on the phone.

"Faaantastic," he drawled.

"I'll call you back if it's not withdrawn from

collections immediately."

"You do that. Hey, when are you coming back to work? It's boring here with all dudes. No one gets grossed out by my jokes when you're gone."

Trying to keep a poker face, Ava told him, "Thank you for your help. I'll be in contact soon," and hung up the phone before Ben launched into a string of dick jokes to try to make her blush. He did that a lot. Ava handed Charlotte her credit card so she could have a nice paper trail to go along with the receipt. Trigger could pay her back later when his bank account didn't look quite so empty. She'd gained read-only access to it this morning and spent fifteen minutes trying to work out how he lived on so little.

"What are you doing?" Trigger asked, six bags of groceries dangling from his hands.

Ava gritted out, "Charlotte here has been kind enough to let me settle your bill here. Haven't you, Charlotte?" She hated when people were prejudiced, and the people of this town seemed to have a big problem with Trigger. First those guys who stirred up trouble on the chip aisle, and now Charlotte. She was beginning to think settling all his bills was going to be as big a jagged pill as this experience.

Charlotte just stood there glaring at Trig as she handed Ava a receipt.

"You didn't have to pay for that," he said as they made their way to the exit.

She needed to get the heck out of here before she verbally fileted Unhelpful Charlotte. "First step to cleaning up your finances is to stop the interest you're accruing, and the late fees. It's a waste of money. You're just bleeding your income into these little meaningless debts, so today we're going to go from place to place and settle them, and you can pay me back when you get the ranch up and running again.

"Ava, I can pay you back now."

Icy wind blasted her face the second she stomped out the sliding glass exit doors. "What?"

Trigger looked over at a police cruiser, where that asshole who had touched her hair was leaning against the open window, talking to an officer. They were both looking over at Trigger with hateful glares.

Trig cleared his throat. "I think we need to talk."

"Yeah, clearly, I need to know what's actually going on here. I thought I was coming in to clean up your finances, but I get a feeling every settlement will be just as difficult as Unhelpful Charlotte made it in there!"

Trigger snorted and pursed his lips against a smile.

"This isn't funny! What's going on? If you can pay me back now, why haven't you settled these stupid little debts already?"

"Because they won't let me, Ava. Not because I can't afford to pay them back."

Her mouth flopped open. "You have fourteen cents in your bank account."

"Because I hate banks."

"Whyyyy?" she asked through clenched teeth.

"Because that asshole's mate runs the bank," he said, jerking his chin at the hair-touching douche-ball. "I keep cash."

"Then why are you living on beans?" she asked, her voice echoing across the parking lot.

"Because I like beans, and it was the end of the week. We haven't made a grocery run in a while because it's a miserable experience," he explained, jamming a finger at the grocery store. "I ain't exactly welcome around here, Ava. And most weeks I want to hole up at the ranch and get through my work—it is a substantial amount of work, I promise you that—and not deal with these turd biscuits in town."

She gave an unexpected laugh at his insult and then tried to recompose her face to look severe.

"What?" he asked, his dark eyebrows low under his cowboy hat.

"You said turd biscuit. I can't keep up a serious conversation if you use insults like that."

"My point, Ava, is that some people in this town want me hurt. And the biggest way to hurt me is by hurting my ranch. There's a dozen of those debts, and I have just as many debt collectors calling me every day. You think I haven't tried to settle them all? I have. There is more going on in this town than you know."

Those words felt like a slap, and the smile fell from her face. "That's the problem, Trig. There was always more going on than I was allowed in on. You think I just left because my dad was a deadbeat? Because I wanted to escape? I wouldn't have wanted to so badly if I wasn't always on the outside here. Explain now."

Trigger inhaled deeply, relaxed his shoulders on the exhale, the grocery bags dangling at his thighs. He shook his head and glared at the police cruiser. "I can't give you the answers you want."

It stung. His denial stung. She'd thought they were in a different place, but here was the famous Trigger shutdown. And just like when she was a kid, she got hit with that insecurity. She wasn't cool enough to let in on the town secrets. Outsider, outsider, outsider, that's what she was, right? That was her destiny.

Her eyes burned, and she blinked hard. "I'll find a ride back to the ranch," she murmured as she walked away.

"Where are you going?" he called.

Pissed at him having this much control over her emotions, she ripped out her to-do list and jammed it up in the air. "I have shit to accomplish." Good and angry, she fumbled for one of the thirty pens she kept in her oversize purse. She had to click it three times because her mittens kept getting in the way, but finally she marked off:

Grocery shopping
Snow boots and warmer jacket
Settle the general store bill

Settle the bar tab at the GutShot

Trigger squinted, as if trying to read it from way over there, but Ava just shoved it back in her purse and made her way toward the row of clothing shops down the street. Snow boots next, and then she was going to the bar.

"You can't fix everything, Ava!" Trig called.

"Watch me!" *Oh, ye of little faith.* She would show him. The grocery store was *the tip* of the iceberg. She jammed her pointer finger in the air and repeated out loud. "The tip!"

She heard the ridiculously loud engine of Trig's truck roar to life, and good. He should leave. She was mad enough to breath fire, and she would barbecue his ass if he talked to her right now.

She was neck-deep in her fury, slipping and sliding down the sidewalk on the other side of the parking lot, when Trigger pulled up beside her. The man didn't get the hint. She wasn't some girl whose anger was short-lived, no. She got embarrassed, hurt, and then she had a long fuse that burned slowly. He was barking up the wrong damn tree if he was looking to make amends right now.

"Go away," she said, refusing to look at him as he coasted right beside her.

"Get on in the truck, and we'll talk about this. Talk about why your face is so red and you look pissed off."

"Hard pass. I want to be left alone right now." These shoes hurt. Her ankle almost went ninety degrees twice as she hit ice on the sidewalk, and she was cold thanks to the windchill, but she would die of hypothermia before she got in that truck right now.

"You're stubborn, Ava Dorset."

And there went that fuse. "Takes one to know one!"

"I didn't use stubborn as a noun!"

"Aaah!" she shrieked. And because her rage was infinite, she scooped up a handful of snow, packed it quick, and chucked it at his open window before she could stop herself. Only she missed the direct hit to that jerk-faced ninny, and it hit the edge of the door and exploded all over Trigger's face. The truck skidded to a stop, and whoa, now *he* looked mad. His eyes were fiery and bright, and his face had twisted into something fearsome.

"You want to know what's going on?" he growled

in a gravelly voice.

Ava crossed her arms over her tits. "Yes."

"You really, really think you can stomach the truth behind this town?"

"Yes!"

"Even if it involves your brother? Even if it involves everyone you grew up with? Even if it will change your entire view on the world? Even if I know—*know*—you'll wish you could go back and realize ignorance is bliss? You still want me to spill it?"

Well, that sounded fourteen percent intimidating, but she stomped one shoe in the snow, nearly rolled her ankle, and firmly nodded once. "Yes."

Trigger took off his hat and tossed it in the passenger's seat, then ran his hand down his snowy face. "Fuck!" he said so loud his voice echoed down the street. "I have to do this in phases."

"Great, more stalling."

"Phase one," he gritted out, ignoring her pop-off. "Get you some goddamn shoes that won't kill you. Two! We'll go to the bar. That's next on your to-do list, right?"

"Well, yes, but I don't know how you read that

from so far away, and anyway—"

"Three! I can't just tell you what's wrong with this place. I have to *show* you, and I need Colton's help for that."

Trig put his phone to his ear and stared at her with the angriest expression she'd ever seen on a man's face.

"Who are you calling?" she asked.

"Your brother."

"Why?"

"Because if you're going half-cocked into that bar, I want back-up. Get in the truck."

Part of her wanted to flip him off for telling her what to do, but a bigger part of her wanted to straddle his lap and grind against him right now until he didn't look so mad. She didn't really know what that said about her other than she was turning into a sexual deviant around Trigger. He was this animalistic, dominant, dangerous but protective man, and she liked that shit. He was hot when he was mad, and double-hot when he bossed her around. She hadn't ever liked anyone telling her what to do, but when he bossed her, she wanted to save a Harley and ride that damn cowboy.

She would never stroke his ego like that though, so she kept those horny sentiments to herself and lifted her chin primly and strode slowly around the front of his truck. He watched her the whole time with narrowed eyes, and a little piece of her felt triumphant for annoying him.

But when she opened the creaking truck door and slid onto the leather seat, he immediately shrugged out of his jacket. And as he talked into the phone, telling Colton to meet them at the GutShot, he laid his warm jacket over her lap, and something awful slithered through her middle—guilt.

He wasn't bossing her to be demanding. He'd wanted her in the truck so he could do this—tuck his jacket around her legs and point all the heater vents right at her. And when he hung up the phone, he huffed a steadying breath and asked, "Is your ankle okay?"

Ava's anger evaporated like fog on a sunny morning. "I'm fine."

He gripped the steering wheel with both hands and stared forward. "Thank you for what you did in there. I should've been appreciative. I watched you argue with that old battle ax, and you didn't back down until that debt was paid. For me."

"It's my job," she murmured, staring out the window at the scenic mountains that surrounded the town.

Trig huffed a humorless laugh and rolled up his window. "Charlotte runs with the Darby Clan. That's who those guys were that wanted trouble."

"Are they an MC?"

"They used to be the Devil Cats. Now they're somethin' worse."

Ava stared at his handsome profile as he stared out the front window. A man like Trig couldn't be pushed, or he would disappear like a ghost, or shut down like of piece of rusted machinery. He would go still and quiet and never open up again if she got impatient. She was coming to realize he was a lot like her. So, she waited, because if this was reversed, Trig would have to wait for her to be good and ready to talk.

"I told you they're animals," he murmured. A car honked behind him, and he lifted his blazing gaze to the rearview mirror and eased his foot onto the gas and out onto the main road. "Well, I meant it. They aren't like other men. This town's chock full of men who don't make sense anywhere but here."

"Bad men?"

Trig nodded. "Not because they woke up one day and had the devil in their soul. Bad because they were born that way. Born with fire lickin' at their hearts, and sometimes it gets hard to fight when there is so much darkness in a man. You understand?"

"Is it like that for you?"

"Yes," he said, no hesitation. "I'm made up of mostly fire. It's always been like that. It'll always be like that. This town is full of monsters. You can't take off down the street like you just did. Darby's different than when you lived here. It's got more shadows now, and those shadows have their attention on you."

"Are you the shadow?"

"Not this time." Trig looked over at her, then jerked his chin to something out the window. There was a bench outside of a bootmaker's shop, and on it sat one of the men from the store. The nice one. Kurt. He wore a deep frown but was relaxed, one long leg stretched out, the tread of his work boots caked in snow. His eyes were right on her.

"He'll be tailing you now."

"Why?"

"Because he ain't got no choice. Chase is his boss, and he has a lot of pull in this town. And Kurt has a boy. A little one. If he minds Chase's wishes, the boy gets protection, and around here, that's worth more than gold."

"Why did you stop being friends?" she asked, completely disturbed by being watched.

"He was part of my club, and when I dissolved the MC, it put his kid in danger. Family first with men like him." Trig's voice softened. "For men like me. Kurt had to find someone who offer his boy protection, and Chase can do that."

"Chase is the one who touched my hair?"

"Mmm hmm. He's the leader of those boys and trouble down to the marrow in his bones. While you stay here, you stick close to me, you hear? No runnin' off. I know you're used to independence, but that don't exist here. Independence makes you rogue. Independence puts a target on you."

"You're independent, and so is Colton," she murmured, beginning to understand.

Trigger trapped her in that golden gaze of his and offered her a sad smile. "Exactly."

TEN

The GutShot wasn't at all what Ava had expected. From the name, she'd imagined a forest and hunting theme—dark wood floors, pictures of trees, old rifle décor, and taxidermy deer and wild boar heads on the walls. This place was beer keg tables, eclectic mix-and-match chairs, and an antique green bar with a row of chrome and black motorcycle seat chairs along the front. Eight men sat on the bar stools, and each was currently looking right at her and Trig.

"The fuck are you doing here?" a balding man in his mid-fifties with no less than four missing teeth and a paunch said from behind the bar. He wasn't looking at her, but at Trig instead. Eric, she remembered from when she lived here before. He used to run the three-screen movie theater in the middle of town.

"I'm here to get the lady a beer, boys," Trig said smoothly. "Not lookin' for trouble."

How many times did he have to reiterate that? Every time he came into town?

The bartender's frosty green eyes narrowed suspiciously. "What kind of beer?"

Uh, beer was gross. "White Zinfandel?" she asked through a bright smile.

"Dammit Hairpin! You brought some hoity-toity rich bitch in here?" Eric asked rather loudly and rather rudely.

"Jesus," Trig muttered, guiding her toward an empty space at the end of the bar. "Eric, call her bitch again, and I'm gonna rip your balls through your belly-button. Don't fuckin' test me with it either. Been a whole day since I Changed."

"No, it hasn't," Ava whispered, taking a seat on the stool. "You wore different clothes yesterday. The plaid shirt. You even wore a different cowboy hat."

"Not what I meant, Ava," Trig growled.

"I don't have white zinfan-whatever," Eric deadpanned, his arms locked against the counter.

"Can you just make her a glass of wine," one of the men on the other side of the bar called out. "Anything you got. Hell, it ain't like she's picky, obviously." He was pointing at Trig.

"I think you're the rudest batch of men I've ever met in my life," Ava told them. Yep, that Dorset rage was rearing its mouthy head again.

"Thank you!" slurred a man at the other end of the bar top.

"Oh, shut up, Wade," Eric said. "I cut you off two hours ago. What are you still doing here?" He swung his gaze to the man sitting beside Wade. "Bill, I swear if you've been sneaking him your drinks, I'm going to throw you out right along with him." Eric was busy making some sort of drink with about a half-dozen liquors and a teeny splash of coke while he was griping at Wade and Bill. "Here." He slammed the drink down in front of her, splashing the bar top with a third of it.

"That's not wine. That's a Long Island Iced Tea," Ava pointed out.

"It's a GutShot special. Drink this or nothing, Hoity-Toity."

Eric plopped a maraschino cherry into it and

turned back to Wade to yell at him some more about his life choices.

"You don't have to drink that," Trig gritted out, looking back at the door.

Ava shuffled her brand-new snow boots on the sticky floor and shrugged as she took a sip. It was strong as hell but still drinkable, and shopping had made her thirsty. A couple of the guys down the bar she recognized from the grocery store, and from the way Trig kept casting sideways glances at them, he was well-aware, too. "I need to settle my tab," Trig said to Eric in a deep, take-no-shit voice.

Two of the patrons laughed, and Eric looked at Trig like he'd lost his damn mind.

"Now, why in tarnation would I do that, Hairpin?" Eric asked. "Then the game would be over."

"So?" Trig asked.

"So the game will never be over."

Trig sighed and flicked his fingers at Ava, who was currently slurping loudly on the remnants of her yummy Long Island. "This is my friend, Ava. She is from here, but she left a long time ago to make something of herself."

"Yep," Ava chimed in helpfully. "I'm a—"

"Lawyer," Trig interrupted, looking Eric dead in the face.

"A...lawyer," Ava whispered lamely in agreeance.

Eric arched a bushy silver eyebrow. "A lawyer."

"Yes," she murmured, thinking fast. Sitting up straighter, she cupped the glass in front of her and raised her chin. "I don't normally waste my time on paperwork for a two-hundred and sixteen-dollar bar tab, but since you seem to be playing a game with this man's life, I think I'll make an exception just for you. Let him settle his tab and call off the collectors, or I will drag your ass through a legal fight I assure you, you are not ready for."

The bar got so quiet she could hear the beating of her own pounding heart.

"Get to the GutShot," one of the men from the store said into his phone. "Gonna be blood soon."

Trigger was staring at him, shaking his head slowly. His eyes looked like they were glowing in the bar lighting, but it might have been because his face was getting so red. That, or the Long Island was kicking in mega-quick. He looked downright deadly, every muscle tensed in his body, but his hand stayed gentle on her lower back.

"Let's go," Trig said low.

"Yeah, run, Hairpin," the man with the phone said through a feline grin.

Trigger slapped down a wad of cash and an extra ten-dollar bill. "For my tab and my girl's drink."

She should feel scared right now, not flattered, but... "You just called me your girl."

Trigger's glare faltered and arched from behind her to her face. "What? No, I didn't."

"You did, too."

Trig looked truly taken aback. "I think you heard me wrong—"

"I liked it," she blurted out, then slapped her hand over her mouth because apparently Long Island Ice Teas could talk.

"Aw, that's just what we fuckin' need," Cell Phone yelled. "He's brought in a damn breeder, and now this town will be crawlin' with his kind."

"Don't call her a breeder," Trig said in a dangerous tone.

"A breeder? That sounds barbaric, and he didn't bring me in. I'm working a job."

"How long does it take to incubate one of his little demons?" Cell Phone asked Eric.

"About six months."

"So two more Hairpins running around by this time next year. Fuck no to this." Cell Phone swung his gaze to Ava. "You need to leave."

A long, low, terrifying rumble emanated from Trigger and vibrated against her skin. "Well, you had a shot of us leaving before you got disrespectful with the lady. I told you, she ain't a breeder. And we'll leave when we're good and ready to leave. She hasn't finished her wine yet."

Heartrate tripping, Ava studied her empty glass. Well maybe there was one tiny slurp of Long Island left. She made it loud and then pushed the empty toward Eric. To Trig, she murmured, "Now I'm done, and maybe we should go."

"Nope, I want to play pool all of a sudden," Trigger said, his eyes little slits as he stared at Cell Phone. "Go ahead and bring the Clan in. Go ahead and go for blood. I'll paint this entire bar with red if you try." He snarled up one side of his mouth in disgust and made a tick sound behind his teeth. "Breeder. You've lost your goddamn mind. Look at her, Otis. Look! This ain't her home, and I ain't her man. It's not her job to pop out cubs for me. Y'all have two choices now that this little bar tab game is up. Let us play a game of pool, and fuck yes, the lady will be picking the next song on the jukebox. Call off your pussy cats, or I'll bring in the fuckin' Peacemaker and we'll go to work carving y'all up like Thanksgiving turkeys. Eric, your windows look mighty breakable. Expensive as hell, too. I'd hate for you to have to spend all the money I just gave you replacing them and cleaning up blood, but fuck it, I'm in a mood, and I wouldn't mind smelling copper."

"The Peacemaker ain't welcome in here," Eric rumbled in a voice that had gone gravelly and scary. The green of his eyes looked strange now, too— lighter and brighter.

"What's wrong with everyone's eyes?" Ava whispered, feeling dizzy.

Cubs, Changes, six months...blood. The smell of copper. He was talking about blood. She didn't like blood much.

"Maybe we should go," she murmured, tugging on the sleeve of Trigger's shirt.

But he only leaned over, pressed his lips onto her hair, his attention still on the assholes sitting at the bar. He gently eased her out of the chair, but then shocked her when he swatted her ass, and then he went gentle again as he pushed her toward the pool table near the wall. Trig made his way behind the bar. He yanked open a fridge and pulled out a bottle of cheap white wine and a couple beers, popped the tops of the brewkies with a snap of his fingers like those bottle caps were nothing, and then he jerked his chin toward the door where Colton sauntered in. "Peacemaker is welcome in here because I fuckin' say he's welcome in here."

"Aw shhhit," Cell Phone, aka Otis, said, shaking his head and looking sick.

"Tab's paid, boys," Trigger said in a booming voice. "The game is up, and we'll be coming in for visits whenever the urge hits us. Call Ava a bitch or a breeder again, and I'll let her brother loose on you, and I'll clean up the scraps."

"She's the Peacemaker's sister?" Eric snarled.

Colton sauntered over toward Ava, cracking his neck this way and that as he did. "Eric, did you call her a bitch?"

Her brother, or the Peacemaker, or whatever he went by nowadays…looked different. His face was twisted into a feral expression, and his eyes…

Something was very wrong here. Her brother wasn't right anymore. He reminded her of...Trigger. And perhaps the magic of the liquor suicide she'd just slurped down gave her super-powers, but she was pretty sure this entire bar smelled of manly odor and fur. Fur. Actual fur like when she was a kid and had an Irish wolfhound that would come in stinking like wet dog after a rain.

And there was something else, too. Something just above her senses as the men on the stools stood one by one and began to approach the three of them. It was something heavy in the air that sat on her shoulders and filled her chest with cement and made it nearly impossible to draw a full breath. It was like someone was sucking the air out of the room.

"Colton?" she whispered as Trigger eased her behind his back. "We should go."

But as she peeked out from behind Trigger's gargantuan back, her brother turned a bright gold gaze on her and growled out, "Colton ain't here."

"Oh," she squeaked out. "Amazing. I'll just pick a song on the jukebox then."

Those two were definitely getting broken noses tonight. Stitches perhaps, too. Already she was tallying the cost of medical care for the boys and wishing those damn wild boys would fight a little less and walk away a lot more.

As she turned to high-knee her frightened ass toward the jukebox, Trigger slammed the bottle neck of the wine against the bar, scaring Ava half to death. Bright side though, the others hesitated in their approach.

"For you," he murmured chivalrously, handing her the broken bottle.

Ava took it and held it in front of her, staring at the jagged edges of the glass. "Um, what if there are glass shards in the bottle now? I have a sensitive stomach."

Trigger snorted and then handed her a plastic cup off a stack at the end of the counter. "Pour the wine in the cup."

"And use the bottle as a shank?" she asked.

"Good girl."

"I don't think I would be good at prison," she murmured. "I really wouldn't. Communal showers aren't my gig, and I like cooking with bacon grease and sleeping on a nice mattress, and when we were kids, my dad told me and Colton that prisoners only got bread and water for meals and that sounds very bland and very boring."

"Ava," Trigger muttered. "You aren't going to prison. Drink your wine and go pick something annoying on the jukebox."

She scoffed. "Annoying? Just what kind of music do you think I listen to?"

Trigger wasn't paying attention, though. Instead, he was giving his attention to where the "Peacemaker," aka her dipshit brother, was talking to the crowd of delinquents in the middle of the bar.

Fine. The Thong Song it was. Jerk.

The music player didn't have the Thong Song, but it did have Achy Breaky Heart, and the chorus of groans that filled the air behind her made her evil-smile.

"You need to get your boys out of here," a masculine voice said right at her ear.

"Aaah!" Ava skittered away and glared at Kurt, who'd apparently come in through the back door right beside her. It was still swinging closed and snow was drifting in on the wind. Kurt's shoulders were dusted with the white stuff as he moved around the pool table toward the front door. He didn't take his eyes from her though, and there was something in them. Something that pleaded with her, confused her. He was giving her a warning.

"Trigger, I want to go," she said.

Trig looked at her over his shoulder, but his eyes weren't in the realm of human anymore, and suddenly she felt like the ground was opening up under her, wider and wider until it would swallow her whole.

Cubs. Secrets. Always on the outside. Gold eyes and snarls in chests. Copper. Copper. Copper. House rule. Stay inside at nights. Ava backed up step-by-step until her shoulder blades hit the wall. Trigger watched her like a predator watching prey. *Don't give him your back.* Stay inside at nights. Where had Trigger gone in the snow? Where had his clothes gone? *You know. You always knew. You just didn't want to see what was in front of you.* Secrets. Whispers. Strange things were always happening here. Animals were always being killed by wolves, mountain lions...bears. *They're not men. What are they? They're animals. Colton's not here.*

Ava gripped the neck of the wine bottle and winced at the stinging pain. Red welled up on a long slice down her finger. *Drip. Drip.* Smelled like copper. Copper and fur and something she still couldn't figure out. Something heavy.

"Trigger?" He was close now. So fast, he'd made his way to her. There was commotion behind him, but she couldn't see around his massive shoulders. The air was colder, and there was a breeze. The front door was open, and more and more voices sounded. Colton's voice rose above the others. He was spewing cusswords right along with them. So loud. Her blood was roaring in her ears. "Trig?" she asked again since he wasn't responding. All he was doing was standing inches away from her, staring down at her bleeding finger. *Drip, drip.*

His gaze churned with gold fire, and his lips curled back, exposing straight, white teeth in a wolfish smile. "You said you liked when I called you 'my girl,' but you don't know what that means yet."

The noise was getting louder. Was it yelling or her heartbeat? Trigger knocked the bottle from her hand and let it shatter on the floor. He angled his head like some predator calculating his prey, and then he did something that shocked her to her core. He raised her hand and kissed her wrist right over her tripping pulse. Kiss. Kiss. Nibble. Bite. He clamped his teeth down so hard, he nearly broke skin, and she gasped at the sensation of pleasure and pain. And then he released her and drew her bleeding finger into his mouth. He slowly stroked his tongue over and over her cut until her knees wanted to give way and her body wanted to belong to him.

So much noise. So much, but she couldn't take her eyes off Trig. He looked wild. Untamed. He looked like a demon with those blazing eyes boring into hers as he sucked the blood from her finger. He pulled away slowly and gave her cut a gentle kiss. "I want to bite you so bad, Ava. I want to ruin you. Wreck your life and make you stay right here. I want to get you stuck with me. One bite, and I could keep you, and the devil inside me wants that. He begs for it." Why was he smiling while he said such terrifying things? Chills were lifting the fine hairs on her arms. She should run, but instead, Ava took an involuntary step forward.

The yelling was getting louder.

"I'll give you a choice," he rumbled in a gritty voice. "But before I do, you'll see it all." Trigger leaned forward slowly and pressed his lips to hers.

His hand went rough in her hair, and he kissed her like she'd never been kissed. It was like meeting a storm and having her breath taken away by the wind. Raw strength and confidence meets beauty, and she was scared of how much she felt, but she didn't want him to ever stop either. He pushed his tongue into her mouth once...twice, and then he pulled back suddenly and spun. There was a crack of power like a lightning strike as his fist connected with a man's nose. He was so fast, so confident in his movement, as though he'd thrown a punch a hundred times before. Perhaps he had.

There were three men on him, pummeling, pushing, fighting. But Trig pulled the violence away from her before she even had to edge out of the way. Time and time again, he drew a quick glance to her, as if he couldn't help himself.

She couldn't see Colton, but she could guess where he was. Right in the middle of a surging crowd of men, throwing hits so fast their arms blurred.

"Oh, my God," she whispered, shocked at the sheer violence the bar had erupted into.

She had to do something. For a split second, time slowed as she reached for her cell phone in her back pocket. The police could stop this. They could stop these men from hurting her boys. *My boys. Mine.* But Trigger wasn't struggling. He was laying bodies at his feet like they were sacks of stones. He was making his way through the crowd, working toward her brother. The Peacemaker. What a bullshit name. He had a man pinned by the shirt against a table and was pummeling his face. He wasn't bringing peace. He was bringing complete destruction. Colton was the Warmaker.

Chairs broke, tables buckled, men grunted in pain, and Trig hadn't bluffed about the front windows as he tossed one man out of it like a rag doll. The sound of shattering glass brought time back in line. She couldn't call the cops. The boys might be defending themselves, but they were laying utter waste to the ruffians in this place. Both of them had rap sheets. Both were outlaws. She couldn't be the one to make it worse.

"Trigger, Colton!" she screamed just as red and blue flashing lights lit up the front windows. "We have to go now!"

But she could've been speaking in sign language for all the attention they paid her. There was no reaction to her demand, and desperate times were calling for desperate measures. She should leave and save herself from being arrested right along with them, but she couldn't make her feet turn to the exit. "Fuck," she murmured in a shaking voice.

Ava yanked a pool stick off the table and ran toward where a man was wailing on the back of Trigger's neck while he fought another. With a screech, she pulled that pool stick back and slammed it into the man. But he didn't flinch. He did something horrifying instead. With fiery silver eyes, he peeled his lips back over teeth that were too sharp, and he screamed in her face. Only it wasn't a human scream. It sounded like an animal.

"Don't!" Trigger yelled, rounding on him, but the man fell to the floor, and his body just...exploded. It morphed into something new. Something terrifying. A massive mountain lion lay crouched, all its muscles tensed, just feet away from where Ava stood frozen.

"M-m-m-m..." she stuttered, her heartbeat pounding double-time in her ears. Her skin tingled with the urge to run, but she couldn't move. "Trigger," she whispered, but he was being dragged away by five men, and Colton was screaming something she didn't understand.

"Ava!" Trigger yelled.

"No, no, no! Trigger, don't Change!" her brother roared. And that's what it was, a roar, but the importance of that came secondary to what the mountain lion did next.

It bunched its muscles and rocketed off the floor, right at her, with such speed and agility, she couldn't step out of the way fast enough. A scream caught in her throat as time slowed again. Impact was like an avalanche. Her breath was knocked clean out of her as she slammed back onto the floor, and then there was excruciating pain. A ripping ache like she'd never endured. Not when she'd cut her neck on a barbed wire fence when she was seven in an ATV accident. Not when she'd broken her arm falling out of a tire swing. Not even when her heart had broken in two when her dad left. This was pain that she would never forget.

It was the scratch of claws so deep they etched into her collar bone, and in desperation, she yelled out Trigger's name one last time as the lion's jaws opened and those impossibly long canines came for her throat.

Through the air, an old Colt Single Action Army, her dad's old Peacemaker, sailed end over end in a big arch and landed in Trigger's hand. Eyes blazing with fury, he swung that old pistol quick, aimed, and pulled the trigger.

Boom!

The cat's teeth barely touched her neck before he was blasted sideways, and he scrambled off her with a scream of pain.

The click of Trig pulling the hammer back echoed in the new silence that had descended on the bar. Ava clutched her bleeding shoulder, wincing at the burn of the claw marks. Everyone had stopped fighting at the sound of the weapon.

"Whoa, you shot him in the ass," Eric said from behind the bar where he was holding a bat like he was ready to hit a homerun.

"That was on purpose," Trig snarled. His voice couldn't even pass for human anymore. "The next one goes between the eyes, Chase. I don't care who the fuck you think you are. Alpha? Bottom of the Clan? Don't matter. You were gonna bite her...weren't you, you sick fuck? You were gonna make her Clan. Claim her as your cougar? Fuck that. You could've killed her. You get that, right? And even with a bite, she'd be at my ranch in my clan. Don't matter her animal, so you best get that dumbshit idea out of your head real quick. Change her like that, and I'll let the devil out of me and bury your entire Clan. Every last one. I fuckin' dare you to underestimate me." The seven-inch barrel of the peacemaker was steady as he kept it aimed at the mountain lion. "We're leaving."

"No, you're not," an officer said from the doorway.

"Self-defense and we have witnesses," Colton said from behind Trigger. He jerked his chin at Ava, who was struggling to her feet. "My sister's got claw marks on her neck, and I'm pretty sure this town don't need no more attention on the supernatural shit that's been going on here. She's human, and she's mouthy as hell, and she don't back down an inch. That comes along with being a Dorset. You want to piss her off and let her find her voice?" Colton nodded and dared him, "Lock us up then."

The dark-haired officer clenched his jaw so hard a muscle twitched there. He cast one hard look to the back door and gritted out, "Get on, then, and don't come back to the GutShot again."

Trigger snarled up his lips in a terrifying grimace before he eased the hammer down and handed the old pistol back to Colton. "Lead on, Ava."

He didn't ask if she was okay or anything. He really was telling her to walk herself out of here, but she figured out why real quick. Trig and Colton flanked her, covered her back as she made her way to the exit of the GutShot. She felt like she was a newborn filly on unsteady legs as she bounced this way and that.

"It's the adrenaline," Trigger said low as he held the door open for her.

Her shoulder hurt so bad, and there was warmth trickling down her fingers. "Babe?" Why did she call him babe? She'd never called a man that. The world was spinning like a top. "I don't feel so good."

Her legs buckled, but Trigger's hands were already scooping her up. He brought her flush to his chest, held her tight. He was warm, and she felt safe, but at the same time, this was awful. How embarrassing to fall apart in front of her brother and Trigger. She wasn't that girl. She was tough, but here she was, going to pieces on the small, snow-covered back porch of the GutShot, the wind stinging her cheeks and freezing the water that was welling up in her eyes. She angled her face away from Trigger in shame.

"This don't make you weak, Ava. It's a lot," Trigger murmured, like he knew the exact thoughts she was wrestling with right now. "You're doing good."

Just that tiny bit of sympathy, that tiny bit of support, meant so much, and she turned and slid her uninjured arm up his neck and squeezed as she buried her face against him. His gait was smooth as he walked them down the porch stairs and toward his truck. Was that his lips against the top of her head? There was a soft growling sound in his chest, and besides the pain, that small terrifying sound was part of the problem.

"Are you like them?"

"I'm nothing like them," he murmured.

"I mean are you a...a..."

"Mountain lion?"

Her voice barely came out a whisper since she was shaking so bad. "Yes."

"No."

"But you're something more, right? More than

human."

"I'm not a big cat shifter. I'm something much worse." He sounded sick saying that.

"It ain't worse," Colton said, sounding pissed. "It ain't."

Steeling herself, she pulled her face away from Trigger's warm chest and faced the biting wind so she could look her brother in the eyes when she asked, "Are you like Trigger?"

The color of his eyes said yes. They were gold like the sun instead of blue like Dad's eyes. His cheeks were tinted red, but from anger, the winter wind, or from shame, she couldn't tell. He spat red in the snow, thanks to a split lip, and he nodded as he reached for the passenger's side door handle of Trigger's old Ford. "I am. Chase was almost your maker tonight. Trigger's my maker. That's all I'll ever say about it." He opened the creaking door and then turned and walked away, his boots making deep prints in the new fallen snow. She and Trigger watched him go. He looked so alone with the evening clouds churning above him, his set of boot prints by themselves in the snow, his shoulders hunched against the whipping wind. He didn't look back.

"I'll never forgive myself for that," Trigger said, and there was a ghost in his voice. "He wanted to come see you, Ava. He would've moved where you were just to keep a relationship. But I messed up, and I tethered him to this place. I hurt a lot of people. I ruined lives. I ruined your brother's the most. You should know that before you start calling me 'babe.' That hole you feel in your family? I did that."

Ava's face crumpled as Trigger set her gingerly on the seat. She shook her head over and over and wished away the last ten years. She'd made mistakes, Colton had made mistakes, and Trigger had made mistakes to get them all here. But somehow, they'd all ended up in Darby to make things right or go to hell together.

A part of her wanted to get back in that little prop plane and leave this place. Pretend mountain lion men didn't exist. Pretend she hadn't watched her brother's face get bloodied or clawed, or watched Trigger stand over her and pull a trigger to protect her. Part of her wished she could go back and have her world righted again. Go back to her simple, safe life and never worry about the people she cared about here. But a bigger part of her...the part that had

163

grown loyal over the last couple of days...was relieved she finally knew. Scared, but relieved.

There was a soft ripping sound as Trigger pulled open her clawed-up jacket to look at her shoulder. It hurt so bad she just wanted to go to sleep and not feel anything.

Trig sighed and murmured a curse, then he leaned forward, popped open the glove box, pulled out flask, and told her, "Drink half."

"This is full," she argued, shaking it to hear the sloshing sound. "Plus, I don't think you're supposed to have booze in your truck like this."

"Woman, I've done way worse shit than carry a flask of whiskey in my truck. Drink it. Trust me, you want to."

"Okay." She got brave and chugged the burning liquor. As it seared its way down into her belly, warming her as it went, Trigger opened her jacket wider and dumped the rest on her claw marks without warning.

She screamed, but cut off the sound so she could feel brave. Slamming her head back on the head rest, she closed her eyes and dislodged twin tears to her frozen cheeks. Her teeth wouldn't stop chattering as he poured the last couple drops on her cuts, and she had to clench her hands to keep them from shaking.

"You did so good, babe," he murmured, a slight smile at the corners of his lips.

"You called me 'babe,'" she said, feeling too drained to care whether it was dangerous to fall a little more for Trig. He'd kept her safe tonight. He'd shot a cougar for her. He'd fought for her honor. He was helping her now. Bad boy, good man.

"I'll give you a choice," he said, leaning over her to turn the truck on. As he turned up the heat, he reached under the seat with his other hand and pulled out a first-aid kit. "When I was a kid, I was rough on my body. A tree climber and always falling out. Always getting scraped up. Playing with knives and cutting myself on accident because I wasn't a careful kid. My dad gave me choices when I was hurt bad enough. Keep the scars or he could fix them so they were faint. He would tell me, 'Boy, our life is made for scars.' He was an animal like me. A monster. A good dad, but a monster. He would always tell me by the time I grew up, I would be all scarred up like him. He was covered because he was a rogue. Always fighting. He had to so he could keep his territory."

"Like you?"

"Like me, and like Colton. He said my body would be a canvas that told my story. But I had options. Some cuts he could sew up, patch up, and make into small silver scars that I wouldn't even notice eventually. Those were the embarrassing ones. The ones where I fell out of a tree but didn't learn a lesson. Or wasn't careful enough and cut myself washing dishes. But some he would encourage me to keep. My first fight with a mountain lion." Trigger pulled the top three buttons apart on his plaid shirt and exposed his taut chest. Under the tattoo ink there were four long, shiny scars.

Ava ran a light touch down them, tracing each one. "He didn't sew these up, did he?"

"No. I didn't start that fight, but I ended it, and he wanted me to remember it. I'm good at stitches. Your cuts are clean and short, and they won't bleed much more. I can stitch you up and make them tiny silver scars that you will hardly notice in two years' time. Or...you can let them heal like this, own what happened to you tonight, never forget the danger of the Clan, but also never forget how brave you were, because I saw you, Ava Dorset. You had fire in your eyes and cracked a pool stick over the alpha of the Darby Clan just to protect the back of my neck. You were a beautiful badass. I'm good with whatever you choose. Neither makes you weak."

Ava sat there, aching arm cradled to her stomach, searching his beautiful, flame-gold eyes. She lifted her hand and hesitated just before she touched his dark beard, then found her bravery and brushed her fingertips down his jaw. Trigger rolled his eyes closed and sighed as though it felt good. As though he'd never been touched his whole life. And in this moment, she knew it was going to be very, very hard when she left Darby to go back to her old life.

Now...everything had changed.

She leaned up and sipped his lips. Just tasted them, and his hand went soft when he cupped her cheek. That same hand had pummeled men's faces to protect her and Colton tonight, but for her, it was as soft as a butterfly's wings. Gentle giant for now, but she knew there was something big and dangerous sleeping inside of this man. She knew she should be afraid, but fear didn't exist inside of her right now— only the certainty that she'd never felt this strongly for a man.

His tongue made gentle strokes just past her lips, and time went on and on. She hurt less. Maybe it was the whiskey, or the cold, or maybe it was the drugged sensation she got when his lips were on hers—she didn't know. All she knew was inside that bar, she'd never been so scared, but out here, in Trigger's care, she'd never felt safer.

"Trig?" she murmured against his lips.

"Yeah, Ava?"

She ran her knuckles down his beard and whispered, "I think I need the scars so I don't ever forget tonight."

A slow smile stretched his face. "Good girl."

ELEVEN

Ava fingered Trig's jacket he'd laid over her lap in his truck. "We can't go to the hospital because they would ask too many questions about where I got a claw mark like this, right?"

"That's right," Trig rumbled, eyes straight ahead on the road back to the ranch, hand draped over the steering wheel like a professional snow-driver.

It had been a long time since she'd driven in weather conditions this bad.

"And that was Chase...the...alpha? The one who turned into a mountain lion?"

"Alpha of the Darby clan, yes. They're close-knit, like a family."

"And animal-men are called..."

169

"Shifters. Most shifters group up. It's safety in numbers because we're territorial. Whole clans can get annihilated if they're not careful." There was a dangerous edge to his voice on that last part.

"Are you going to go after them?"

"He hurt you," Trig said simply.

"So that's a yes?"

He inhaled deeply, his nostrils flaring with it, and slid his big, strong hand under the edge of his jacket and over her thigh. Her body's reaction was instant. Warmth dumped into her middle, and her back arched against the seat. She sidled closer until his fingertips brushed the inside seam of her jeans. He squeezed her hard. Not hard enough to hurt, but hard enough to let her know he could take charge on a second's notice. Holy moly, he was sexy.

"You'll have questions, and I don't mind answering most of them, but on some things, I'm going to stay quiet so you can't get in trouble."

"Like when you go after the clan."

"Yes. Like then."

He was keeping her out of trouble, so if the cops asked her what happened, she wouldn't be lying when she said she didn't know anything.

As much as she wanted to be Bonnie and Clyde right now, she did appreciate him taking care of her in a small way like this. He was going to quietly defend her, and maybe she didn't want to know what kind of revenge he was probably planning in his head right now. But it meant the world that he was going to avenge the hurt she'd endured tonight.

"You're making me loyal. You know that, right?"

He massaged her leg and then dragged her closer until her hip hit the seatbelt and stopped her progress. "Explain."

"My dad couldn't even stick around for his kids. Couldn't stick around for me. I hated men. He was supposed to take care of me, and he didn't. So, I grew up swearing—*swearing*—to never care about someone so deeply again. Especially not a man, because men were leavers."

"Colton never left."

"No, but he was checked out. Nineteen-year-old kid raising his little sister? I ruined his youth. It was clear, and I felt like a burden. Sometimes I thought he worked extra shifts just to get away from me."

"Nah, he was having trouble keeping the heat on. I picked up a part-time job just to help him. He was overwhelmed, but never checked out. You're his family."

Feeling brave, she slid her fingers over his on her thigh and squeezed his hand. "I don't understand why he wouldn't tell me that. I spent my last few years here thinking he hated me for making him grow up too fast."

"It wasn't that, Ava. You had trouble with some of your classes in school. Trouble making the grades. Colton was making it as easy on you as possible to focus on school and get the life you always talked about wanting. His focus was on keeping you in the house you grew up in so nothing else changed for you. But he was a kid, and all of a sudden, he had guardianship and big bills, and he did have to grow up immediately. And he did. For you. He was busting his ass trying to keep life as steady as possible for you."

"And you were, too?"

Trig huffed a laugh and nodded. "Hell yeah. I was breaking up sheetrock for a construction company and laying tile to help y'all out."

"Why?" she asked, baffled why a nineteen-year-old kid would give his money away so selflessly like that.

"Because you were Colton's family, right?"

"Yeah."

"Well, you both felt like mine to take care of, too."

She was taken aback. This overwhelming urge to cry and hug him took over her. "I was wrong about so much."

"Nah, everything happened the way it was supposed to happen. Regrets are pointless. Look what you did with your anger and disappointment. You went out and became a dragon. You run your own business and don't take no shit from nobody. You know how many women I've seen buckle under your kind of start in life? Not you, though. Never you. I never had a single worry about how you would turn out, Ava. Little spitfire, and stubborn as a hair in a biscuit. I fucking love that about you."

Butterflies flapped around in her stomach at his mention of the L-word, and feeling even bolder, she unbuckled her seatbelt, scooted all the way over on the bench seat of his truck until their shoulders touched, and then she re-buckled herself into the middle seat.

He lifted his arm smoothly over her shoulder and

tucked her against his warm ribs, then smiled down at her. Sure, his eyes still couldn't pass for human in any way, but that smile leveled her insides and eased a tension in her shoulders she hadn't known she was carrying. He was okay, and she was okay, and everything was going to be okay.

The Long Island and the whiskey had done its job. The edge of the pain in her shoulder was nice and fuzzy now. Trigger had taped gauze to it, and if she didn't move her arm, it was fine. When a country song she recognized came on the radio, she smiled. It was about a first date.

"Was tonight our first date?" she asked.

"Woman, if I took you on a date, you wouldn't be questioning it."

"Well, you took me shoe shopping. And we grocery shopped together. And we got in a barfight together."

A deep chuckle reverberated from Trig's chest. "You want our first date to include a barfight?"

"Well, who else could say that about their first date?" She clamped her teeth gently onto his shoulder, and a soft groan sounded from him. Whoa, sexy man. She did it again, and he rolled his hips slightly.

Ava slid her hand to the seam of his pants where his hard erection pressed against it. She couldn't help the smile that took over her face if she tried. She'd done that—made him want her back, like she wanted him.

It was warm in the truck, and the snowy woods were blurring by outside the window, but she was completely taken by his relaxed profile. His knuckles were still bleeding, but he looked the epitome of calm.

"Usually, I'm worked up after a fight and I need to Change right away. Sometimes it's really bad, and I Change during a fight."

"You seem okay right now."

Trig frowned. "I am. You confuse me. Half the time you make my animal harder to manage, and the other half you make him quiet and watchful. Tonight was close. I almost Changed in that bar, and if that ever happens and you're around, you have to make me a promise."

"Anything."

"Promise me you'll run."

"Leave you in a fight?"

"Yep. Leave me, leave Colton, leave the fuckin' town until you know I'm Changed back. No hesitation, just get the hell out of there."

"What are you?"

He brushed his lips against her hair. "I'm a weapon."

"A weapon?"

He pulled to the side of the road and pushed the gear shift on the steering column all the way up into park. "I'm the trigger. It's why my dad gave me that name. Anyone messes with someone I care about, I get obsessed and don't back down until they pay. I can't back down. I don't have it in me."

"Trigger," she whispered, and then repeated because she had to know, "What *are* you?"

He leaned into her and kissed her deep, and when he pulled away, he rested his forehead against hers and murmured, "I'm yours."

It wasn't the answer she'd expected. It was so much better. Someday he would show her what dark creature dwelled inside of him, but for now he was giving her something just as big. Himself.

She only winced a little when she cupped his cheeks and kissed him. And the pain dulled even more when he laid her back on the bench seat and pushed his tongue past her lips. His fingers dug into her hip, into her thigh, into her knee, and back to her thigh as he touched her rough, how he wanted. She loved this. Loved how he couldn't seem to control his hands around her. It was the perfect amount of pressure to rev her up. Already, she was writhing against him, needy sounds in her throat as he kissed her senseless. She remembered exactly what his fingers felt like sliding inside of her, and right now, she wanted—no, *needed*—that so she could feel centered again. She'd been floating off the ground since she'd watched Chase turn into a big cat, but Trigger could fix it. He could give her relief. He could anchor her to the world again with his touch. He could make her forget her fear from earlier and she could get lost in him, and right now, she didn't want anything else.

He shoved her legs apart and laid his full weight on her. She should've been uncomfortable under such a big man, but it was fine. The pressure made her feel safe. His kisses were becoming more urgent, and she ignored the pain when she lifted the hem of his shirt. He reached over his head and yanked his shirt off, shoved his jacket out of their way, unzipped hers, and lifted her sweater. And then he did something she fell in love with. He laid down on top of her and let off this sigh of relief when the skin of their stomachs touched. He was so warm, and she got that same sense of happiness touching him like this, too. He was the perfect fit for her.

The roll of his hips was smooth against hers, and his hard erection was rubbing her in the perfect spot. There was a soft rumbling sound in his throat that gave her chills. Desperately, she reached between them and unfastened his belt. Trig's hips jerked as she popped the button of his jeans. God, he was beautiful, propped up on massive, tattooed, locked arms, his triceps flexing as he looked down at her. His gaze and touch were flames against her skin, and all she wanted...the only thing...was for him to be buried deep inside of her, connected. This wouldn't be like her first time. This would be even bigger. She didn't know how she knew, but she just did. Tonight, he was letting her in. He was letting them build a bond.

She'd never felt so close to another person in her entire life, and she was high on the thought that she wasn't alone anymore. Trigger had been the most unexpected thing to happen to her.

Hands steady, he undid her jeans and pulled them along with her panties down her hips to her knees, then past her ankles. His focus stayed between her legs as he pushed the head of his cock into her by an inch. He drew back and lifted that gold gaze to hers, watched her face as he gripped her hip and pushed all the way inside her.

God, it felt so good. She arched her back and let off a helpless sound, spread her knees wider for him as he withdrew and pushed in again. How could anything feel this incredible?

"Trig," she whispered as he pushed all the way in again, bumping her just right as he did.

Lowering himself to her, he made her feel safe and secure as he kissed her and bucked into her faster, faster. No taking their time on this one, and she didn't want to. Already, she was close to climax, the pressure building and building until she was yelling with every stroke. "Right there," she pleaded, and he kept steady as her body shattered.

Big, rutting, dominant man. He milked every aftershock until she was twitching, and then he eased out of her and flipped her over like she weighed nothing. It hurt staying propped up on her one arm, but his hand went gently around her throat, and locking his other arm right beside her, he helped her stay upright in the sexiest damn way she could imagine. It was a gentle choke. She could still breathe just fine, but having his big hand right there, holding her in place as he slid into her from behind had her gasping his name.

The growl in his chest filled the cab of the truck, and the windows were all steamed up. She slammed her hand against the passenger's side window as he bucked into her over and over, faster and faster. His hand went from her throat to between her legs, and he touched her clit as he stroked into her. His teeth grazed her ear and she lost it. Again. She cried out as her climax came out of nowhere, and Trig reared back, then slammed into her deep. He froze for a second as his big dick pulsed hard inside of her, spilling warmth. A dozen more strokes, and he'd emptied himself into her, and their throbbing releases matched.

"Oh, my gosh," she whispered, rocking back and forth with his leisurely pumping motion. That had been...everything. She never wanted to be disconnected from him. She could've stayed just like this forever. For two songs, it was bliss. It was a hand print on the steamed-up window, warm air from the vent, and soft country music. It was her man behind her, taking care of her body with slow strokes, making her feel safer than she'd ever felt. It was the dull ache in her arm that reminded her he'd finally let her in on this town's secrets and drawn her from the outside right into the center of the circle. It was snow falling in the high beams, and his soft kisses on her shoulders, the back of her neck, and her ears. He was adoring her and making her fall for him even harder.

This was that life-changing moment when she knew she would never be the same. Not after tonight. Not after all she'd seen and done. Not after being with him like this.

After tonight, there would be no leaving Trigger easily.

TWELVE

What had he done?

Trigger eased his arm out from under Ava and stared at her in the dark. She was curled on her side, the blue moonlight highlighting her beautiful face, her dark lashes lying on her cheeks as she slept soundly. How could a woman feel so safe to let her body go unconscious around a monster like him?

What had he done?

He'd been so good as a kid, was unselfish and let her go make a life for herself. But now he was forming a bond with her. Testing her. Tethering her to him. To this place. To this town she'd been so uncomfortable in. And she'd come back, and look at him now. He'd let himself lose control with her twice now because he was weak around her. Because he needed to touch her and hear those sexy little noises while he made her feel good. He'd been getting more and more attached to her, and then seeing her under Chase's teeth had done something awful to him. It had scared him and made him desperate to make sure she was okay. Alive. Breathing. Warm under his touch. He'd taken her rough, and what had she done? Loved it. He could tell just by her body's reaction. By the sounds she made, encouraging him. She'd awakened a monster, gained his fealty, and what good did that do her? None at all if she was still leaving next week.

She was it for him. Always had been, and now that he'd had her, he wanted to keep her for always. He couldn't stop staring at the rips on her shoulder, the slices that had caused her pain. Those claw marks represented his life. His existence was pain, and look what had happened to her just a few days in.

What had he done? He'd ruined himself. He'd wrecked his damn heart, and he would spiral bad when she left. He would Change uncontrollably and mourn the loss of his mate, and his soul would always feel a little darker. And it would always feel like he was carrying his heart outside of his body. That pain would never go away. He knew this. Knew that's the way it would be because that's how it was for shifters when they picked their person. It was permanent. There was no take-backs, and what the fuck had he done to both of them?

He'd ruined them.

He rested his elbows on his knees and ran his hands over and over his hair, unsure of how to feel. It was hard to regret being with the woman he'd thought about for so long. It was better being with her than he'd imagined. And he, hardened bear shifter, loner, Clan of One, outcast of Darby, and ruiner of her brother's life, had an even weaker moment and imagined her holding his cub. Imagined her looking down at his little dark-haired baby boy, her neck arched gracefully, curves fuller from getting his son to air, humming under her breath and rocking back and forth on the front porch swing he'd carved with his dad all those years ago.

Goddammit, he wanted that more than anything, and he had no right to it. His body felt like someone had just shoved a saber into his guts. His body tensed and tingled in waves, and he knew he was on his way out. The grizzly was giving him warnings. Vacate quick because the monster wanted the body soon.

He'd never hated what he was so much until now. She deserved normal, and he could never be that. Oh sure, he could keep her body safe. She had the protection of a beast. But he was the biggest risk to Ava's happiness. A flash of memory filled his head...the vision of Colton's body after he'd mauled him. The night he'd Turned his best friend. What would keep him from doing that to Ava?

On the end table sat a notepad with numbers scrawled all over the top page. Trig grunted in pain as his body jerked with the need to Change. Soon now. Soon he wouldn't exist, and the bear would be roaming the ranch, causing havoc.

Doubling over the pain in his center, Trigger scribbled a note to Ava so she would know exactly what happened when she woke up and he was different toward her.

Dear Ava,

I've never been scared of anything until you came along. What happens if I lose it? What if I bite you and make you a monster like me? Or worse? What if you don't survive me? The animal isn't a blessing, it's a curse, and the longer you stay here, the deeper you sink into that curse.

The clan calls me Hairpin Trigger.

To you, I'm Quicksand.

You're safe from everyone but me,

Trig

THIRTEEN

Three days. Three days of waiting for this dang claw mark to heal, three days of sifting through mountains of paperwork, trying to figure out a way to make this place viable again, three days of Colton staying conveniently off the ranch, and three days of Trigger being too busy to even talk to her in passing.

She'd woken up to a letter that she'd read a couple dozen times, trying to understand what had gone wrong. Trigger had shut down on her, gone cold, and the sting of it was like a slap on frozen skin.

The boys had been so close-knit in the bar, moving as one, and she'd been a part of that. She'd felt it. She was theirs to protect, and now she was theirs to ignore?

The small dining room was where she'd set up shop. It was a closed-off room, not open to the kitchen or living area, and she used the hand-carved dining table as her desk. She'd picked the chair on the end because right on the corner of the table was an old scrawled carving of a TM. Trigger Massey had been naughty when he was a kid and used some sort of pocket knife to do this. But for Ava, sitting here tracing those little initials while she talked on the phone to settle and consolidate his debts...well, it was a way to feel close to him. Because right now, he felt very far away. Her chest went hollow just thinking about it.

She'd gone through her life so afraid of being close to anyone, especially a man, and then her heart had landed on the most dangerous one of all. One who harbored some unknown animal, but even scarier, who drew her attention and made her imagine a life she had no business imagining.

Ava looked at the dark wood walls and the little shelves with the mismatched white and blue teacups. There was a small fireplace near her with crackling flames keeping her warm. It was snowing outside, and the evening shadows were covering the ranch, but in here, it was bright and cheery and warm. So why did she feel so cold inside?

Three days had given her plenty of time to work through what she'd witnessed and experienced in the GutShot. She'd even gotten a book from the Darby Public Library on shape-shifters, but none of the lore seemed to match up to what she saw and heard of the mountain lions.

Through the dining room doorway, she could see the heavy steel front door, and it made sense now. Trigger was keeping the monsters out. But perhaps the monster he was trying to keep out...was him.

Her life in Alabama seemed very small and vanilla compared to what was happening here. She'd left Darby to find an exciting life, not knowing she had enough excitement to last her four lifetimes right here.

The old baby-puke brown corded phone on the wall rang, and she pushed away from the table and answered it. "Hello?"

"Yes, is this Two Claws Ranch?" a woman asked.

"It sure is. I'm Ava, what can I do for you?"

"Well, I come through on vacation every couple of years with my family, and a few years ago we did a trail ride through your ranch, but I'm looking on the website, and it says it's no longer booking those. I had the best experience, and my husband actually re-proposed to me up on one of the mountains. I wanted to re-book that experience, but it looks like you are shut down. I thought I would call and just see if you could make an exception, or maybe ask if you were just temporarily shut down? We're staying a couple nights in Darby next month."

Ava's mouth was hanging open. "A...trail ride?"

"Yes, ma'am, a couple of good lookin' cowboys took my family on a two-day excursion and told us the history of the area. Cooked out for us and set up our tents and everything. It was an experience my family has been talking about for two years."

"I'm new here," Ava explained, "just started last week, so I wasn't around for the trail-riding part of this ranch, but is it okay if I asked how much Trigger charged you?"

"Trigger! That was his name. He was real quiet but real polite and was really good with my boys. And yes! I think total we paid eight hundred dollars for four people, and that covered everything."

Ava stretched the cord as far as it would go and

sank down into her chair as a light bulb went off above her head. Scrambling for her notepad, she shoved the scribbled top page out of the way and asked, "Well, I think I could convince Trigger and Colton to do another trail ride depending on when you're in town. What dates were you thinking?

"Oh, my gosh, this is amazing. Um, February six and seventh if you have those dates available."

Ava scribbled the dates down, asked for her email address and number, and then said she would talk to the boys and call back as soon as possible. And when she hung up the phone, she leaned back against the wall and whispered to herself, "Why the hell didn't they tell me?"

Detective hat on, she sat down to her computer and clacked away at the keys until she found the Two Claws Ranch website. It was simple as hell and needed some major overhauling, but yep, there it was. Information about trail rides. There were one and two-day excursions, prices, and an outline of what it entailed, everything. Holy motherfuckin' hell, she was going to kick both boys in the shins for keeping this from her.

She'd been wracking her brains for a solution on

syphoning income to this place and paying down the debts so Trigger could get some relief and get out of the red. But he wouldn't get paid for his cattle at auction until the spring, and something had happened to the herd that cut them way down right before she came. He'd lost a lot of his profit right there, and this place was turning into a money pit.

But a trail riding company? For tourists passing through? Heck yes.

Reinvigorated, she closed her laptop and made her way into the kitchen, head full of ideas to get this place up and running again. She only had a week left, and it didn't sit well with her to leave this place worse off than she found it.

Half distracted, she browned some hamburger meat with chopped onions and added stewed tomatoes, tomato sauce, and beans, then sprinkled all the spices she wanted on top and went to work on cornbread in a cast iron skillet. She let the chili simmer for thirty minutes while that cooked, all the while planning and plotting.

This could work.

The door opened so fast it banked against the wall, but it wasn't Trigger's fault. If his surprised expression was anything to go by, the wind had kicked up and yanked it from his hand.

She couldn't, however, take her horrified gaze off his bloodied face. The left half was covered in crimson, and there were dark stains on the shoulder of his jacket. She yanked the chili off the stove and rushed over to him, but he winced away from her touch when she got too close to a gash on us head, right under the brim of his hat.

"What happened?" she asked on a breath.

"Best you don't know."

Her fury was instant. She shoved him in the chest. He hadn't even made it inside yet, but she pushed him again. He allowed it, eyes averted as he backed his way to the front porch stairs.

"I'm right here, and you're leaving me out," she said. "You're pushing me away, so how does it feel, Trig? I made you food. I spent time on it, and if you don't eat it, I'm gonna be boiling mad. I'm trading you, though. You sit out here in the fucking cold until you decide you can talk to me like I deserve. Think real hard about this while you're out here—there's a girl inside that warm house who likes you and who isn't scared by the shitstorm half of your life, who has hot food waiting in there for you and who wants to clean your face and hug you and forgive you for whatever sins you did today." She jammed a finger at him. "Appreciate what you got, Trigger Massey, or you won't keep it." She strode inside and slammed that steel door as best she could, but the damn thing was heavy and thudded softly into the frame.

Ignoring the front door, she busied herself by cutting up cornbread in that cast iron skillet. She buttered it and dished up two bowls of piping hot chili, and then she set that two-seater table and stood right by it, locked her legs, crossed her arms over her chest, and glared at the door. Not three seconds later, it swung open, and there was Trig, arms locked against the frame, mouth set in a grim line, still bloody as hell.

"Chase won't be messin' with you anymore."

"Did he do that?" she asked, gesturing to his mauled face.

His eyes tightened at the corners. "Some of it."

"Did you go after the whole Darby Clan?"

He dipped his chin once.

She heaved a breath and licked her lips. The fury left her voice when she said, "Well, tell me you won, at least."

A slow, surprised smile stretched his face and reached his tired eyes. "I always win."

She huffed a laugh and shook her head. "Ridiculous man, is this what I should expect from a life with you?"

His grin faltered, but came back softer. "Yeah. It won't change. I am who I am."

"If you won't budge, then you can't ask me to change a single thing either."

"Wouldn't dream of it. If you changed anything about yourself, you wouldn't be perfect anymore."

"Oh, I'm far from perfect."

Trig stalked her, boots clomping on the wood floors, scattering chunks of snow as he approached. He took off his hat and tossed it on the couch and shrugged out of his stained jacket.

"I eat too many children's snacks," she admitted through a grin.

"I love children's snacks." Another step closer.

"If it's cold, I'll probably wear socks while we're having sex."

"We can match." Another step.

"I had three pet goldfish die on me in a year, and I

think I'm bad at raising animals."

Trig frowned. "Okay, that we're going to have to work on. Don't touch any of my livestock with those fingers of death."

When she swatted him, he chuckled, then pulled her into a hug and lifted her feet off the floor. Her back cracked in several places from the pressure, but it felt good.

"I want a baby reindeer and seven baby goats, and I'm going to dress them in pajamas and make them all social media pages and they will be my hairy children."

Trig snorted. "Not until you learn to stop killing everything," he murmured against her ear, resting the uninjured side of his face against hers. "Babe...I'm sorry."

"Well, do it right and apologize properly. Tell me why."

"I got scared and I ran. With you, I feel different, and for a man like me, it's dangerous. I need a steady life, or as steady as it can be, and you came in here like a stick of dynamite and blew everything I thought I wanted to hell."

"I gotta short fuse," she teased.

"Woman, no one's arguing that. You gotta temper on you. I fuckin' love it. I love watching you straighten that little spine of yours, stick them tits out, chin up, glaring your prey in the eye, and daring them to talk back to you. Stubborn, territorial, moody, beautiful, feisty, flawless woman. I wish you weren't such a perfect match. I wish you couldn't manage me so well, because then next week would be easier."

"When I leave?"

His beard scratched against her soft cheek as he nodded. "I've been counting down already. I get sicker by the day, and steering clear of you only makes it worse. Feels like I just wasted our time."

"I have an admission, and I don't want you to look at me while I say this because I'll chicken out. But you should know what running does to me. You should know so you can fix it. I know you don't want to change anything and you're a creature of habit. You're set in your ways. But I also know you care about me and you don't want to hurt me. So, this is how you stop that. Ready?"

"Ready."

She inhaled deeply and hugged his neck tighter, legs still dangling off the ground as she clung to him, so she crossed her snow boots at the ankles and began to admit something really hard. "Do you know what always hurt the worst when I lived here before?"

"Your dad leaving," he guessed.

"No. That did hurt, but it was how everybody treated me after. Colton was struggling to take care of me when he was still a kid himself. I understand better now what he went through, but it doesn't change the fact that he couldn't be there for me like I wanted. I was lonely. No mom, no dad, my brother was checked out. And then everyone around me treated me like I was on the outside. Like there was this big secret everyone knew but me."

"And now you know it."

"But can you imagine what that feels like, Trig? To be shut down on?"

He pressed his lips to her cheek and then nuzzled her right there. "Yes. The whole town shut down on me."

"Yep, I can see that. So now you can understand how hurt I get when you shut down on me. What it feels like. You should try harder not to let me feel that way. You started building something really good with me, and then you slammed the door and went cold, and dammit, Trig, I'm already scared. You get that, right? This is scary."

"I won't hurt you. I won't let the animal hurt you." There was undeniable oath in his voice.

"It's not the animal I have a problem with. It's the man. I think about you too much. Even admitting this stuff feels like weakness. I've never shared myself with another person. And all I want to do is hole up in my little shell like the clam I've become and block you out. But that's not courageous. It's cowardly, running from something that's real."

"You're scared of liking me?" he asked low, rocking her gently as his hand cupped the back of her head as though she was precious.

"Yeah," she whispered.

"I'm scared, too. Not for me. For you. I want better than what I can give you. I want to be better, and I get scared I won't cut it. Look around, Ava. This is the life I can give you. Cracked log walls, a leaky roof, me out working the ranch all day. Fighting because the animal in me needs it. A steel door to keep me out of here when I'm not in my right mind. Your brother living next door with a half-rabid squirrel. Danger every time we go into town. Danger here. An animal I can't control like I want. And then I think about...what happens in a year, or two years, when you miss your old life. When you got my baby in your arms and you're watching him Change for the first time, and it rips your guts out because it hurts him every single Change. And you gotta watch your baby fall apart over and over. You gotta watch your man do the same. My mom couldn't handle it. She left when I was three because she couldn't deal with the animals. Couldn't deal with the dangerous life. What happens when that claw mark on your shoulder becomes two. Or three. Until you're painted in them? What happens if..." He swallowed hard.

"What happens if what?"

"What happens if I make you an animal like your brother? If I make you an animal like me? I know what that kind of guilt feels like, and it's enough to buckle a man. I carry that guilt for Colton, but carrying it for you, too? I know what I can and can't handle, and hurting you?" He shook his head, back and forth, back and forth, the roughness of his beard a stark contrast to her own sensitive cheek. His voice came out a raspy whisper as he said, "I can't."

She bit her lip so it wouldn't quiver and expose how weak she'd become around him. Ava found steel for her voice when she lifted her chin and said, "None of this is your choice to make. It's mine. I'm not your mom. Your first mistake is in thinking I'm like any other girl. I don't pick my people easily, Trig. But when I do, I'm in it. Give me the next week, no running. Show me what life here could be like so I can make a good decision and not live with regrets or what-ifs. Tell me everything. All the grit in your life. For once, just be completely open with someone. You can trust me. I'll keep you safe. I'll take your secrets to my grave. It's how I'm built. Make me happy, and I'll make you happy, and we'll see if I fit here or in my old life best. Deal?"

Trig clamped his teeth gently on her neck, holding there for a moment before he rumbled, "Deal."

"Good. Now go clean the gore off your face before the chili gets cold. I'm hungry."

He set her down and kissed her. He tasted slightly of iron, and she had to wipe the side of her lips because Trig had smeared her.

"House rule number two because, hell yes, I'm

making rules now, too," she called after him as he sauntered into the hallway toward the bathroom. "If you get into fights, you need to clean up before you start making out with me. I don't want to taste blood on you."

"You don't mind my rules," he argued. "We told you to stay inside at nights, and what did you do that very first night? You were standing on the front porch screamin' my name like some sort of banshee. Probably caught the attention of every predator around."

"Well, I was trying to catch the attention of the biggest predator. You."

Over the running water in the bathroom, she could hear him chuckle. "You should be running scared, Ava."

"I've decided I don't like running much anymore," she called as she set out napkins by their dinner. "Plus, I read in a library book you aren't supposed to give a predator your back."

"Give me your back, and I'll fuck you from behind."

Ava's eyes went round, but by the time he came back in, drying his face with a dark gray washcloth, her smile was downright Grinch-worthy. She liked his filthy mouth. And now he looked a lot less like a corpse and a lot more like the man she was falling in love with.

"I have ideas," she murmured.

He pulled out her chair for her. "I bet you do."

He liked that she was a go-getter. She could tell by the way his eyes danced when he said that.

"I got a call from a lady about a trail ride today."

"Whoa, whoa, whoa, wherever this is going, it's a no. Colton and I tried that before, and it was a nightmare."

"Why?" she drawled.

"Because running a business is not for me. Getting people to actually pay was a pain in the ass, Colton was in charge of packing the animals with provisions, but he's horrible at it, and on each of the three rides we conducted, I was worried I was going to Change at any moment and eat the riders like little people-kabobs. It almost happened on the last one. For the safety of unsuspecting tourists, we put that business to rest."

"Okay, those are the problems, and here are some solutions. Running a business isn't so bad if you have some training on how to do it. We could set up your Two Claws Trail Rides as an LLC, set up a way to pay on the website, do half down at reservation and half due before you leave on the trail. I can teach Colton to pack because organization is totally my thing, and with the Changing thing? Well, you're going to have to figure that out. Maybe be a pinecone for a whole day before a ride so you don't have the urge or something."

"I'm not a pinecone shifter." He bit off half of his buttered cornbread and stared at her thoughtfully. "What's an LLC?"

"I could get it totally set up where no one could steal your company name and you could get paid by customers under that name for tax purposes and you could have a professional, trademarked trail-riding company. I can have a logo made and build from there. Because I've seen what you make at auction on a good year with a full herd, and you don't even have a full herd of cattle this year. It won't even cover expenses to keep this place running. You'll sink within the year if you don't plug up the leak in your boat and start bringing income through the ranch. It'll take me two days to set up the business. I can revamp the website, look at provisions you need for trail-rides, the works. We can do this right."

"We," he repeated.

"Yeah. Like a team. Team Save-This-Place."

"You really think we can?"

"Yeah, but you have to make a big move, one that's a little risky, or this place, and your dad's legacy, will fold."

"I ate the cattle."

"I eat cattle all the time. I love steaks, hamburgers, hamburger helper, and barbecue," she said, ticking them off with her fingers. "And I also like—"

"No. Ava, listen to what I'm saying. I actually killed a good part of my own herd. I had no control. And you're asking me to risk human lives to do these trail rides."

"The other day I watched your eyes turn bright gold, you smelled like fur, and you had a growl in your chest. A man turned into a mountain lion and attacked me. And what did you do?"

"Shot him in the ass-meat with your brother's Colt Single Action Army?"

"Well…yes, you did, but that's not what I meant.

You stayed human."

Trig stopped eating and angled his head, frowning at her. Slowly, he set his spoon down and leaned back in his creaking chair, crossed his arms over his broad chest. "Huh."

"I would say you had plenty going on that could've provoked the werewolf, but you didn't let him out. Can you name a situation on a trail ride that would be worse than watching a shifter try and Turn the girl you like?"

Trig scratched his jaw, his beard making a raspy sound under his fingertips. "No. The woods and predators, I can handle. And I'm not a werewolf."

"And you'll have Colton on the rides, and he didn't turn into a beaver in the bar."

"We aren't beaver shifters."

"It's okay to be a porcupine."

"Nope."

"If you want to teamwork this and try to save this place, you have to step out of your comfort zone. That means self-improvement, bring the bumble bee under control."

With the tiniest eyeroll, Trig shook his head and muttered, "I'll talk to Colton about it."

"So you're going to think about it?"

"Maybe."

"I'll handle all the paperwork and advertising. You try and control your ferret."

"Are you having fun?"

"Kind of. Elephant? Shrew? Newt? But not a tiny newt, a cool one the size of Godzilla? Octopus, and you have the power to strangle your enemies and open tight lids on jars." He was going to get a sore neck from shaking it so much. "Frog? Ocelot? Wereparakeet? Meercat? River Dolphin?"

"Grizzly bear."

"Grriiizzly bear." Holy hell. "As in brown bears? As in the ones with the paws the size of small cars?"

"Not quite. Come here. I want to show you something."

Numbly, she stood and followed him out onto the front porch where he grabbed her hand and pressed it over the deep carvings on the log walls, just below that wishing number, 1010. Even with her fingers spread as far as she could, she didn't even come close to how wide those marks were.

"Oh, my gosh," she whispered, utterly stunned by the sheer size of that paw.

"Joking aside, Ava. I really am a monster, and you can't ever forget that. Not even for a second. Dinner can wait. We need this daylight," he rumbled, disappearing inside as she stared at the injured, splintered wood. Trig returned with a rifle and was emptying a handful of bullets into his jacket pocket. "Go put on some warm clothes. I'm taking you on date number two."

"What's date number two?"

With the sound of metal on metal, Trig shoved a bullet into the chamber. "Teaching you how to kill me."

His boots made hollow sounds on the porch as he walked away, and before he could hurry her along, she took her fingertips off the deep claw marks and touched the wishing number. And under her breath, she said, "I wish I never have to pull the trigger on Trigger."

FOURTEEN

Life with Trigger was good. So good. It was easy. It was fun and romantic in ways she hadn't expected. He did little things for her. Yesterday, he'd bought her a little reindeer stuffed animal in town and handed it to her with a trio of her favorite children's snacks— animal crackers, Cheeto paws chips, and gummy worms. It was better than any bouquet of flowers. It was her love language he had deciphered in record time. She didn't need big expensive gifts. She just needed him to listen and think of her sometimes.

It was the countdown each day that took away from her happiness here. She had her daily planner lying open on the dining table among all the Two Claws Trail Ride business paperwork. It was something she tried to ignore as she set up the business that was a total Hail Mary to save this place. Each day, Trigger opened up more, hugged her, held her hand, talked to her about his childhood, the things he loved, the things he wished for, the life he wanted. He made her laugh all the time. He could be broody when his bear was in his eyes, turning them gold, and he was witty and fun when his eyes were chocolate brown. She had fallen in love with all parts of him, but it was terrifying to admit that out loud. He'd taken her under his wing, taught her how to saddle her own horse again, taken her out on rides, showed her the million things he did around the ranch to keep everything running. He cooked for her sometimes, and she cooked for him others. Each evening before dinner, he practiced shooting targets with her, and when they went into town, he always asked her along and held her close to his side in his truck.

Life with him was comfortable. It made her appreciate taking moments to find peace, because that's what this quiet man did. He observed and pointed out beautiful things. Birds in the snowy brush, an early born calf finding it's legs in the barn for the first time. She was even finding the humor in his hellion horse's attitude.

Trigger was a man who talked when it was important, and he always surprised her with his wisdom. Days were full and perfect and covered in smiles. But each night, when he would go check the animals in the barn one last time, or when he needed to Change, she would go into the dining room and mark through another day in her planner with a red pen.

And each time she did, it was as if she was dragging the tip of that sharp pen across the most sensitive part of her heart.

Three days left, and she didn't want to leave.

Scratch.

Ava put the pen down and closed the planner so she didn't have to see all those marked-off days, and feeling a little upset, she did something she hadn't done since she was a kid. She went to find Colton for comfort.

Clad in a sweater, leggings, and snow boots, she crossed her arms over her chest to ward off the bitter wind and jogged across the snowy lawn to the small cabin that sat just to the west.

Three knocks had her knuckles feeling raw on that wooden door, and then Colton yanked it open exactly three inches. Eyes narrowed in suspicion, he asked, "What?"

"Okay, hermit," she said with a giggle, "let me in. I'm ready to meet your squirrel."

"You called her a rat the other day."

"Oh, my gosh, it was a joke. Now move." She pushed her way in and barely ducked out of the way when a tiny, hairy torpedo went sailing at her face.

Colton snatched the little squirrel out of the air and held her to his chest as she struggled to escape, beady eyes on Ava. "Genie doesn't like being called a rat."

"*Genie* probably needs to be a free squirrel in the wild!" Ava exclaimed, clutching her chest over her pounding heart.

Colton snorted. "I've tried to set her free like eight hundred times. She comes right back. She chewed a hole in my damn door getting back in here. She's loyal," he deadpanned as he put Genie in an oversized cage covered in hanging, colorful toys. She would've been a cute squirrel if she wasn't staring at Ava and biting the bars of her cage like she was rabid.

"She's got an attitude problem," Ava murmured, sinking down onto the couch in the small living area.

"Reminds me of someone else I know."

It would've been more offensive if Colton hadn't relaxed and wasn't wearing a baiting grin right now. He plopped into the old leather recliner across from the couch and rested his boot on the coffee table with a clunk. "You got somethin' to tell me about you and Trigger?"

"I don't know what you mean," she said coyly.

"Hmmm, well he's been humming under his breath, and he is about fifty percent less murdery. Yesterday, I caught him googling baby reindeers for sale on his phone. When I called him out, he asked if it was okay that he likes you. I nearly lost my breakfast."

Giggling, Ava sat cross-legged and pointed to Dad's old revolver. "Is that why they call you the Peacemaker?"

"Nah, that's coincidence. I used to stop Trigger from maiming people who provoked him in town. I was his keeper in a way."

"But not anymore?"

"Now, I'm like him. I want to fight just as much. I

don't keep the peace that much anymore."

"You're loyal," she murmured.

The smile slipped from his face, and her brother rubbed his blond, two-day stubble. "Sometimes loyalty is a curse."

"I don't think it is. I think you got all the things Dad lacked."

His startled gaze twitched to her. "What do you mean?"

"You're a badass, Colton. Look what you did. You raised me the rest of the way when Dad left. You must have been hurting too, but you never showed it. You just worked hard and paid the bills and kept me in school. I used to think you checked out on me, but Trigger told me what it was really like for you." Her voice cracked because this was hard to say. She swallowed a few times and tried again. "You stepped up for me, and I think you step up for Trigger more often than anyone realizes. I think you're still the Peacemaker. Dad was a leaver, but you're a stayer. I'm glad I came back and got to see you for what you are. I was wrong to stay away for so long."

Colton's eyes filled with emotion and lightened to a muddy gold just before he gave his attention to the crackling fire in the small stone hearth. "I wanted to go where you were."

"I know. Trig told me. The bear got in the way, huh?"

His eyes filled with emotion. "It don't matter. The past is the past. It's been good on the soul to have you around here smarting off. Plus, it's been funny as hell watching you try to learn to saddle that old swaybacked nag you keep wanting to ride."

"Hey! She's safe and beautiful. White like a snowflake, and I feel like a queen when I sit on her."

"Well you look like the court jester, but keep imagining yourself royal."

She threw a cardboard coaster from the end table at him as he cracked himself up.

Grinning wickedly, Colton said, "I'm gonna take a picture of you bouncing around on that Shetland-sized pony beside Trig on his black stallion. Y'all look hilarious."

With an eyeroll, she leaned against the armrest and pulled the sleeves of her sweater over her hands. "I came in here to make amends and tell you I missed you, and you've ruined it and reminded me that I don't actually miss you at all."

"I'm gonna sic my squirrel on you if you don't be nice in my house."

Scrunching up her face, Ava grimaced at Genie, who had two tiny hands around the bars of her cage and was staring back at her. That little, furry demon was going to visit her nightmares.

"I have an admission," she said.

"Oh, God, I don't care about your lady time of the month. Just tell me when to throw chocolate at you and leave you alone."

"Ha! I forgot you actually used to do that my senior year. No, I need advice. Like...brotherly advice."

Colton's eyebrows arched up, and he relaxed back in the chair. "Wow. Okay, lay it on me."

"I like it here. I like Trigger, and I like being around you again. I like learning about the ranch. I like trying to save it." She inhaled deeply because it suddenly felt like an elephant was sitting on her chest. "But I built up this life, and I should go back to it. I'm right on the verge of being really successful in my business. I've worked so hard to get where I am, and I thought that was all I wanted and needed. No friends, and no meaningful relationships because those are risky, right?"

Colton twitched his attention to the door and back. "Go on."

"Well, I've been counting down since I got here to when I could leave, and at first I was so happy to mark off the days, but now I hate it. It's one more day I can't have back, one more day closer to leaving, and I don't know when I'll be able to take time off and come back. I had everything figured out, Colt. Everything down to the littlest detail of my future. And then I came here, and now I feel so different. Like...from my bones outward...I've changed."

Colton's face had morphed from confusion to something more while she'd talked. Hopefulness? Pride? But he twitched his attention to the door again, and his eyebrows lowered slightly. "How are you different?" he asked, standing up.

As he made his way to the front window to push the curtains aside, she explained. "I was working sixty hours a week and so driven. Just happy to be working toward a goal, and I thought I was fulfilled, fixing the holes people had dug themselves into, or helping them invest in their future. But I came here, and I work maybe eight hours a day on saving this place, but I get so much downtime to just...be. To spend time getting to know Trigger, spend time getting to know you again. I feel a part of something, and I don't know if I've had that since it was me and you and Dad against the world, you know? Now it's kinda scary thinking about going back to that life I've worked so hard for, and what if it isn't enough anymore? What if I want to take coffee on the porch and watch the snow in the mornings, or pet the baby cow—"

"Calf."

"Whatever. What if I miss the open space and miss dinners actually eating at a table talking to someone I care about? What if I miss you?"

Colton leaned his back against the wall by the window and shook his head sadly. "This place has turned you into a sappy girl."

With a giggle, Ava said, "It really has. I can shoot guns and herd cattle on my little ancient steed, clean a chicken coop and my hands have blisters. I gave a baby cow a bottle, and I feel tougher in some ways, but in others? Feels like I let too many walls down, and now I don't know how to build them back up again. I think y'all broke me."

"You ain't broken, Ava. There's no shame in feeling. What do you want to do?"

"What do you mean?"

"Stop thinking about your business and what you did to get here for thirty seconds, and just ask yourself what would make you have the happiest life." He leaned his head back on the log wall and repeated, "What do you want? Do you want your safe life back at home? You'll probably kill your seven plants within the year because, last I remember, you were shit at keeping things alive. You want your sixty-hour work weeks? You want those TV dinners in your apartment surrounded by paperwork? Because you're bringing your work home, right? You want to keep your shutdown? Keep the old Ava, the one Dad still has power over, because you're still struggling to let anyone in? Or do you look around this place and want something different? This is a dangerous life, Ava. You'll get hurt. You'll get scars. You'll have to stand by while Trig and I make some really fucked-up decisions sometimes. You'll watch your man hurt. You'll watch him struggle with that fuckin' grizzly that never settled inside of him. Do you keep those shallow, emotionless roots you grew in

Alabama? Or do you get loyal and accept your place here, under our protection? Grow them deep, thick roots that won't let go of a place. Do you want to stay alone, or do you want to grow a Clan? Do you want to become royalty? Because that's what you'll be here. You get that right? Trig will put you on the throne of this place and make you queen." Colton shuffled his feet. "I can't make this decision for you, but I can make an observation. I've been watching you. You came in sour-faced and tired. Chewed up by the world and shut down. And over the last week and a half, I watched you smile more, laugh more. Watched you melt against a man when Trig hugged you. It's not my place to tell you whether you should chase a half-life or not, little sister. I can only tell you what I wish you would do."

On the edge of the couch, emotion thickening in her throat, hope stirring in her blood, she asked her brother, "What do you wish?"

"That you'll stay here and give me and Trig something to fight for."

Boom!

The sound of a gunshot was deafening in the quiet that stretched between them. Ava jumped.

"Shit," Colton muttered, reaching for the rifle above the door. "I knew something was off. Get to the big house, Ava. House rule, don't come out of there." He waited for her to make it to the front porch before he yanked the door closed behind them.

"What's happening?" she asked, panicking and stumbling as fast as she could through the snow in a beeline for the big house.

"That was Trig's gun. Bolt that door, Ava, and don't you come out of there," he called over his shoulder as he ran for the barn. "No matter what you see, don't you come out."

Boom! Boom! "Colton!" Trig's voice echoed through the clearing. "Stay with Ava!"

She strained her eyes, but couldn't see where Trig was. It was too dark in the space outside of the porch lights.

A roar filled the air. It seemed to come up from the earth and vibrate through her entire body. It was the most terrifying sound she'd ever heard. It promised destruction.

"Colton!" Trig yelled again. He was in trouble.

"Oh, my gosh," she murmured to herself, hands shaking as she shoved the door closed behind her.

"There she is," a gritty voice said behind her.

With a gasp, she spun and slammed her back against the door in terror. Chase stood from where he'd been sitting on the couch. He was almost unrecognizable from the bruising on his face, but she would never forget his feline smile. It was so empty.

"I didn't get to finish what I started the other day, sweetheart." He limped a step closer, and her blood froze. She couldn't move.

"I've been fuckin' with Hairpin's head for a year now. He's so easy to mess with. Do you know how to topple an apex predator? You don't corner them, nah." His frosty silver eyes narrowed, and his smile turned even colder. "You get in their head and make them go crazy. And when they don't know which way is up or down, you end them and take their territory."

"Why are you doing this?" she whispered shakily.

"Because it's fun to shatter unbreakable things. Trig messed with the MCs. He wrecked the balance here. Took income from my crew. Took income from me. He fought me too many times. Shamed me in front of my own damn people so I found a bear for hire. He's been systematically eating Trig's herd for a year, and all the while Trig thinks it's his bear doing the damage. I can see it. See him failing. See him losing it. See the guilt he carries."

Boom! Boom!

Ava hunched and whispered a curse, tears welling in her eyes.

"You came along and fucked up my game. We were ruining his life, and you came in and started fixing the little secret things like the debts. And then I watched Hairpin Trigger keep his human body when I tried to Change you, and I knew my timeline had changed. You're making him salvageable." He made a clicking sound behind his teeth. "Can't have that. Can't have a bear clan taking roots here. Not when I was so close to ending them. So tonight I brought in that War-Bear I've been paying to fuck with him...and he'll end him. He ain't weak in the head like Hairpin. He's good at killing pathetic things."

Chace was to her so fast he blurred, and his fist came sailing at her face. She only had time to close her eyes and throw her hands up before impact, but it never came. Instead, a tremendous crash sounded. When she opened her eyes, the alpha of the Darby Clan was pulling himself from a broken wall, and another man was standing in front of her. Kurt?

"Find your grit, girl," he snarled over his shoulder. "Your boys are dyin'."

And something snapped inside of her. The fear that had been pouring through her like water from a broken faucet just stopped. She went still. The shaking died to nothing.

Your boys are dyin'.

My boys. My boys. Mine. My Clan.

She didn't react when Kurt hunched into himself and then exploded into a massive mountain lion right in front of her. She didn't react when Chase did the same. They circled each other slowly, long canines exposed and faces scrunched up with the promise of violence.

Find your grit, girl.

Fury took her. Rage, red and infinite, filled every cell in her body until she moved on instinct.

Fuck house rules.

The titan cougars behind her clashed like two freight trains, but they could have their fight. She had one of her own. Ava ripped the rifle she'd been practicing with off the hooks by the door. She grabbed a handful of bullets and yanked the door open.

The biting wind felt like nothing against her cheeks. Her clothes were too thin for the weather, but she didn't feel the cold at all. All she felt was the fire of the rage that Chase had built in her middle.

Eyes reflected in the snowy woods around her. "Cougars, Cougars everywhere," she whispered as she pressed bullet after bullet into the magazine until the rifle wouldn't take anymore. Then she shoved the bolt lever forward and slid one into the chamber. Safety was on, but she could change that in an instant. The Darby Clan was messing with the wrong damn ranch.

Behind her, the sound of shattering glass and splintering wood was deafening, but she had to trust Kurt to keep her back safe while she ran for the sound of the roaring bear.

She ran to the tree line and blasted through it, legs and lungs burning with the effort.

Harley came barreling through the winter woods directly at her, and she barely had time to jump out of the way. When he screamed and locked his legs as he skidded past her, she nearly stumbled over her feet to avoid his pounding hooves. He spun and gave her his back, reared up, exposing the mountain lion holding on to him. Red splattered on the snow. Fuck.

"Harley!" she screamed as two more mountain lions ran through the snow for him. "Scrape him off!" She pulled the rifle tight to her shoulder and aimed for the cats coming for him. She wasn't a good enough shot to take a crack at the one on him without possibly hitting Harley, but she could keep the others off.

The bear wasn't alone anymore. The woods were filled with bellowing predators, so loud her head was filled with the noise. No matter how long she lived, she would never forget the sound of shifter warfare. She didn't have time to think, only react. Pull the gun, safety off, deep breath, hold like Trigger taught her. Aim, brush that trigger, *boom*! Pull that bolt back, shove another bullet in the chamber. Fuck, too close, and the cougar that was charging through the snow was coming for her now, not the horse. She lifted the rifle, but it wasn't fast enough before he was on her. He hit her with the force of a head on collision, and she hit the ground hard. Pain. The roaring in her head was so loud. So loud. The weight on her disappeared, and she opened her eyes just in time to see the cat hit a tree and fall to the snow.

hind legs. The cougars scattered as Trigger let off a deafening roar. And the other bear with the blond fur stood and joined him.

One by one, the mountain lions that remained slunk away.

She couldn't find it in her to be sympathetic that they'd lost. Colton lowered to all fours, his blond fur red over his ribs. Trigger's fur was matted with crimson, and Ava...when she lowered the rifle to her side, could feel the throbbing ache of claw marks and warmth streaming down to her wrist. It would hurt when the adrenaline rush faded away. Through the trees, Harley stomped his front hoof over and over, dragging it through the snow in agitation, his skin twitching, the claw marks on his withers shiny and dark.

Trigger was three times her height when he was standing like this, and even when he lowered to all fours, the muscular hump between his shoulders still towered over her. When he turned, his eyes were still half-empty, his lips snarled back. And then he Changed, right there, right where she could witness how painful it must be, and she understood what he'd meant when he'd said she would watch their sons hurt with each Change. Bones broke, muscles reshaped, and though it was a fast shift, ten seconds maybe, she couldn't even imagine the pain involved.

He went straight to his knees the second he was human. His body twitched and shook, and he was bleeding, but his eyes were only for her. He tried to get up, but he stumbled back into the snow.

She ran to him, set the rifle down, and wrapped him up in her arms. "Trigger, Trigger," she chanted on a whisper.

"Tell me you're okay," he said hoarsely, his hand tight around the back of her neck, his other clutching her sweater in an unbreakable fist. He was rocking them gently back and forth, but he was shaking so bad.

"I'm okay. No one bit me, just scratched."

"Fuck. Fuck. Ava." He sounded gutted, so she hugged him tighter, but he grunted in pain.

"It's okay. Everything is okay. Chase was waiting for me in the cabin, but Kurt fought him."

Trigger tensed. "Kurt defended you? Against Chase?"

"Yes. He pulled him off and Changed right there. They were fighting when I left with the rifle."

"Colton," Trig called. "Kurt switched sides."

"Shhhit," her brother said from behind them. "I'll check on him."

Ava could hear his feet crunching through the snow as he passed, but she'd buried her face against Trigger's neck and didn't want to move.

"Go get his kid," Trigger called after him. "Get him before the Darby Clan does."

"What's happening?" she asked.

God, Trigger was shaking so bad she wanted to take her sweater off and wrap it around him.

When she tried, though, he stopped her. "It ain't the cold. My body hurts after the Change. Doesn't matter if Kurt is alive, or lying dead in my cabin right now, his cub is at risk. Kurt turned traitor on the Clan. He protected you. I owe him. His cub will be under my protection now."

Now she was shaking. Part of it was from the frigid wind and her thin clothes and part of it was the adrenaline crash that was commandeering her body. Or maybe it was shock. She eased off his neck and looked around at the lions in the snow. At the red. Eight bodies. No...nine. Ten.

"Don't look," Trigger rumbled, his voice raw. He

cupped her cheeks and drew her gaze back to his. Shaking his head, he murmured, "You don't have to look, Ava. I need you to go back to the cabin, okay? Can you see the porch light through the trees?"

She nodded, her eyes burning with tears. "Yes."

"Follow Colton's footprints, go straight to his cabin. Take the rifle. You need to warm up. Okay? Your skin is completely frozen. Warm up in Colton's cabin, don't go in the big one. Colt and I will take care of everything."

"I should...I should...help." With what, she didn't know.

"The biggest help you can do is be safe and warm so I can focus on taking care of everything out here. Hey," he said, pulling her drifting gaze back to his again. His voice dipped to a whisper as he told her, "You did so fucking good. So good. Your part is done."

She gripped his wrists and nodded. There was no way in hell she wanted to leave him here, but it's what he was asking, what he needed, so she forced herself to stand on unstable legs.

Biting her bottom lip hard, she bent over and picked up the rifle, made sure the safety was on, and followed Colton's footprints into the dim light.

"Ava."

"Yeah, Trig?" she asked, turning.

He sat there on his knees in the snow, his skin pale and stark in contrast to his tattoos. Blood, mussed hair, golden eyes that held her steady. Warrior. He'd kept her safe tonight. Again.

"I love you, too. Never forget that, okay?"

Her heart had soared at the first part, at his admission of his feelings, but she'd grown confused by the second. It was the grit in his voice that did it. The sorrow.

Her heart ached for reasons she didn't understand as she nodded and promised him, "I won't forget."

And as she left him there to walk back to the cabin, it struck her.

Tonight the Darby Clan had been destroyed.

And in the wake of that destruction, the Two Claws Clan had been born.

There had been a goodbye in Trigger's voice, but her mind was made up.

Shifters. Outlaws. Danger. Pain. Uncertainty. So much work ahead just to save this place. This home.

Love. Protection. Devotion. Loyalty.

Knowing...*knowing*...the boys had her back always.

It didn't matter what she'd done up until this point in her other life. It felt so far away. It only mattered that she owned the life she was destined for, and this felt important. Trigger was important. His story as alpha of this Clan was just beginning, and leaving him would mean leaving her heart in these mountains.

Colton had talked about chasing a half-life, and he was right. She was done with that.

This was her stand, this was her place, this was her home, this was her family, this was her man. This was her life.

This was where she belonged.

FIFTEEN

The fire of Colton's stone hearth crackled and seemed loud in the thickening silence. Genie was asleep in her cage, finally. That little rodent had glared at Ava since she'd come in out of the cold but finally got bored and passed out. Ava was cuddled up on the recliner under a blanket, knees to her chest to keep warm, her arm in full bandages and throbbing despite the pain meds Colton had given her when he fixed her up. He was really good at first aid. Too good, and she'd wondered how many times he'd worked on Trigger, and on himself. Between Kurt and Colton, Kurt's dark-haired little three-year-old boy slept soundly all curled on the couch under a blanket.

It was Kurt who broke the heavy silence. "I'll be

leaving as soon as I heal up."

"You don't have to, you know?" Colton assured him.

"I do," Kurt said, tiredly. He was pale, and his entire torso was covered in bandages, which showed through his unbuttoned flannel shirt. His cowboy hat sat on the armrest right beside him. He looked like he'd aged a hundred years in a night; his eyes were so exhausted.

"Thank you for what you did," Ava murmured.

He gave a half smile and looked down at his son. "I couldn't stand by and watch them carry out what they planned. Can't teach my boy to be a good man someday if I'm not a good man. If I don't try to do what's right. Y'all are good people, just different. Chase never understood that there's nothing wrong with different."

Colton's gaze drifted to her again. He had been watching her for the past hour since he'd come back to the cabin from helping Trigger. Watching her like a hawk on a mouse. He bit the edge of his thumbnail and stretched out one of his legs while she curled down deeper under her blanket. She'd never been so tired in her whole life, but she couldn't sleep until

Trigger came back.

She fingered the bandage on her arm and said, "Colton, just say what it is you want to say."

He pursed his lips and leaned forward, elbows on his knees, hands clamped in front of him. "You don't seem scared off."

She shook her head. "I know I should be. I know that's the normal reaction, but maybe I have the bits that Dad was missing, too."

"Loyal?"

She nodded. "I love Trig. I love you. I want to stay and see this thing through. I want to be here to watch things improve for you. I want to be a part of this story. It feels big."

"You made up your mind then?"

"I'm staying. This is my place. My home." She offered him a tired smile. "This is my Clan."

Kurt snorted. "Two rogue bears and a human does not a Clan make."

"We're outlaws, don't you know?" she asked cheekily. "We don't follow the rules."

The door swung open, letting in the cold breeze. In the open door frame, Trigger stood tall as a redwood, strong and steady again in a flannel shirt, worn jeans, and boots, his hat drawn low over his eyes, but it didn't hide the bright color there. In his hand was something that instantly hollowed out her heart and made her feel empty. Empty and then stubborn. He held her suitcase. He wouldn't meet her eyes when he said, "I've got a prop plane lined up for you. I know it's a little early and we haven't finished the business stuff, but this needs to happen."

Ava shrugged. Numbly, she said, "Okay." Standing, she let the blanket slip to the chair and waved to Kurt.

Colton stood and followed her to the coat rack, and together they dressed for the frosty morning.

"You're taking this easier than I thought you would." Trigger sounded so sad, but what was the point in arguing with him? He was running.

"I scared you last night," she said.

"Very much."

"And you'll always do this, won't you? The back and forth. Wanting to draw me in close, then push me away to keep me safe?"

"If it's me and my life that puts you in danger, then yes."

"Okay."

Trigger turned and walked out to the porch. "I'll wait in the truck."

Oh, he was hurt at how easy she was making this, but he didn't need to be. Ava slipped her feet into her snow boots and grabbed her purse, then led the way out to Trigger's truck, which was smoking out exhaust, already warming up.

Colton waved and said, "See you in a few," and headed to his own truck.

"Where is he going?" Trig asked out the open window.

"To get in his truck so he can give me a ride from wherever you drop me off at."

Trigger's mouth fell open. "What?"

"Hey, Colton?" Ava said.

"Yep?" he asked, walking backward.

"If I asked you to bite me...would you?"

"Gladly," he said through a bright smile.

"Cool, we'll do it when we get back home then."

"What?" Trig asked louder. Now he looked mad.

Ava pulled open the passenger side door, settled in front of the vent, and buckled her belt. "If I'm a bear shifter too, then you don't have to worry about shooing me away every time I'm in danger. And if

Colton bites me, you don't have to carry a single ounce of guilt. And look how happy he is." She pointed to where Colton was performing a drum solo in his truck to some rock music. "He won't feel guilty biting me."

"No!"

"Yes."

"Ava, no."

"Yeeeees," she sang in an opera voice. "Do you want to listen to country or rock music on the way to the airport? There's a hundred percent chance I'll have a headache on the way back from listening to whatever that disaster is rockin' out to in his truck," she said, jamming a finger at Colton again. Probably screamo music from the way his head was thrown back. He was basically howling one long word that she could easily hear from here.

"This isn't how this is supposed to go."

"Mmm, I think nothing is going to be the way it's supposed to go in this Clan."

"We're not a Clan."

"Two Claws Clan. Should I update the website to say that?"

"No! Because we aren't a Clan!"

"Whatever you say, Alpha. Can we get to driving? I'm ready to get back here so I can get some sleep. Last night was a little crazy, what with the war and the bears and the trying to survive and all. Also, I'm hungry. Can we stop for breakfast, or do you want me to wait until Colton drives me back home?"

"Home," he repeated, his eyes round as he searched her face.

She smiled. "Yeah, silly. Home."

He looked over at the big house, where the windows were busted out, the door had been ripped off, and the porch was destroyed from Kurt and Chase's fight. "Home is a mess."

"We'll fix it. Together. And besides. Home isn't a building, Trig."

"What is it then?"

Ava unbuckled and scooted all the way over. "Home is you."

He looked at her like she was the most beautiful thing he'd ever seen, and her stomach erupted with that fluttering sensation she knew he would give her for the rest of their lives. He was so good at giving her butterflies.

Trigger put his arm over her shoulder and drew

her in close, kissed her hair, and let his lips linger there. "Are you sure?"

"Yes."

"Because this is the only time I'm going to ask, and this is your chance to back out. If we do this, you're here to stay. I'll follow you if you leave."

Ava curled up her legs in his lap and nuzzled her face against his arm. "You're mine and I'm yours, Trig. And that's just the way it is. Maybe that's what it always was, but we just fought it. At some point, we have to both pick a path. And for me, it's so clear that my path is you. And Colton, and Darby, and this place. And a future baby reindeer."

He chuckled and hooked his fingertips under the crease of one of her knees. "God, I love you, Ava Dorset."

"I love you too, so quit trying to shoo me away. It's a waste of time. I'm not going anywhere, and you yourself said I'm stubborn as a hair in a biscuit. So...either I can turn into a bear, like you and Colton, or I can stay human, and you can make an oath to me right here and now that no matter what, you'll never push me away again."

Trig couldn't seem to help the smile that kept

curving up his lips. "I get to keep you?"

"You better keep me. I'm very needy, and also I'm gonna get us on track with the trail rides, I have my business to set up here, and I'm going to keep you from eating tourists, and keep that one"—she pointed at Colton—"from adopting more rabid squirrels."

Colton was now staring out the window with a "let's go" expression on his face. He had never been the patient type.

"Trigger Massey, will you share your cans of beans with me for always?" she asked.

He bellowed a single laugh and rolled his head back against the headrest. After few seconds he asked, "I get to choose human or bear?"

"Yep. I trust you."

He looked over at her, and she was just stunned by the easy smile on his face. She'd never seen him so happy, and it banished that hollow feeling she'd gotten when she'd seen her suitcase in his hand.

"Stay human," he said in that deep baritone voice of his. "Stay just as you are, you perfect woman. Human, stubborn, mouthy as hell, sexy, caring, devoted, amazing woman. I don't know how I got so lucky with you, but I'll spend the rest of my life making sure you know you're loved."

Her eyes prickled, and she struggled to keep the emotion from her face. "Tell me you won't leave. I won't ask after this. Tell me this one time, and I'll keep it with me always."

"I ain't like your dad, Ava. You always had me. From here on, no more running. No matter what, it's you and me."

"And me!" Colton yelled out his window. Damn his bear hearing.

Ava giggled and leaned up, kissed Trig good on the lips. She felt so warm, like she was glowing, because this was the happiest moment of her life. Sitting on the bench seat of Trig's old Ford, heaters all pointed toward her because he couldn't help but take care of her, his arm around her, his other hand on her leg, him looking at her like she hung the moon and stars. Colton was leaning out his window, pointing to something in the distance. "Is that Harley? Your demon horse kicked through his stall again, Trig. I'm not gettin' him this time either. He bit me in the ass cheek last week when I tried to bring him in."

Indeed, Harley was trotting around the edge of the clearing as though daring them all to chase him.

And Kurt was standing in the doorway to Colton's cabin, a slight smile on his face.

Home is a mess, Trig had said.

Trig was home, and he was a mess.

Colton? A big mess.

And her? She was perhaps the biggest mess of all. Because she had spent her entire life fighting to be alone and build up walls, and what had happened here? Trigger tore them all down and stomped those bricks to dust so she could never rebuild.

She didn't know how to do this. She didn't know how to be a family, a mate, a friend, any of it. But she was damn sure going to give it her best, and none of this was scary when she was tucked up safe with the man she loved.

Home is a mess.

Damn right it was.

It was her mess.

Keep Reading for a bonus book from T. S. Joyce, the second story in the Outlaw Shifters series, A Very Outlaw Christmas.

A Very Outlaw Christmas

(Outlaw Shifters, Book 2)

ONE

Trigger Massey puffed air out of his cheeks in frustration as he squatted down next to the hole he'd dug under a couple of loose planks in the barn floor. He was running low on his cash stashes thanks to setting up the new Two Claws Trail Rides business. He was one week out from Christmas, and Ava deserved a special present, but until the business started bringing in income, he was strapped for cash.

"What are you doing?" Ava's brother, Colton, asked from behind him.

Trigger didn't turn around. As quick as he could, he shoved the old rusted coffee can filled with dollar bills back in the hole, scooped the cold dirt over the top, and replaced the wooden floor planks.

"I'm gonna fuck this up," he muttered to his best friend.

The creaking sound behind him told Trigger that Colton had settled on the old bench he and Dad had built when he was ten. It was a match to one they'd made for a cluster of shade trees out by the river. This bench was scooted up against the stall next to Harley's. Dangerous territory. God, this place still felt empty without the old man bustling around.

"You're gonna fuck what up? Your relationship with Ava? Nah, she's got stars in her eyes when she looks at you. They say love is blind, and I believe it now. She settled for your hideous ass and moved all her shit into your cabin. You're in. She don't pick her people easily, but when she does, she sticks to them like superglue." He shoved his hands in his pockets and blew out a long, frozen breath in front of him. Then he scrunched up his face. "It's actually annoying. Ever since she came back, she's been trying to fix my life, like it needs fixin'."

"Listen to you bellyachin'," Trigger teased. "For the last ten years, you complained she never came home, and now that she's here, you want her gone."

"Grass is always greener," Colton said. The scars on his face were a stark reminder of what Trigger had done to him five years ago. He was a life-ruiner, and he didn't want to be that to Ava. He wanted to be better. "The grass is greener under your own boots if you water it enough," he said softly.

"Who are you and what have you done with my pissy friend?"

Trigger chuckled and shook his head as he stood to his full height. "Your sister is a force of nature. It's hard for a stone in a river to stay still if the water's pushing it constantly."

Colton narrowed his eyes and leaned back against the stall door. Trigger's pitch-black stallion, Harley, stuck his head out and snapped his teeth about a foot away from Colton's face, but he ignored it. Colton knew exactly how far that asshole could reach with his bite. "Sometimes lately, you remind me of your dad," Colt said. "In a good way."

"Yeah well, he couldn't make my mom happy, and now look what I'll do with Ava. I can't even afford a damn Christmas present like she deserves."

A single bellowing laugh came from Colton. "Ava don't even like Christmas, so you're in the clear."

Harley was repeatedly kicking the stall now, and it was messing with Trigger's senses. Maybe he heard Colton wrong. No one hated Christmas. "What?" Trigger asked, meandering to the bench.

"Oh, she used to be a total elf before Dad left. This holiday was the one time of year that the old bastard tried. He was nice all December, but wore himself out for the rest of the year. We went and chopped down a tree together every year like some lumberjack family, matching in our flannel shirts, and decorated the tree with ornaments from the dollar store. That *I* purchased by the way because Dad was only good at spending money, not earning it. Ava would make hot chocolate every night in December. And she would make this lame countdown calendar and make us go to every stupid parade and celebration and school party."

Boom! Boom! Harley was giving a go at escaping again.

Trigger shook his head hard, trying to get rid of the building headache behind his eyes. "And then your dad left, and it changed?"

Boom! Boom! God, he was glad they'd reinforced Harley's stall.

"Oh, yeah. She became the biggest Grinch. Look around your cabin, man. It's a week to the holiday, and she hasn't put up a single decoration in there. No tinsel, no wreath, no peppermint-scented hand soap. I'm pretty sure you're screwed if you ever want to do Christmas up right. She'll eat you up and spit you out if you even mention getting a tree." Colt wrenched his voice up an octave to mimic his sister. "Trees belong outside!"

Trigger snorted because Colt actually could do a good impersonation of his mate's voice.

Boom! Boom!

"Harley!" They both yelled at the same time.

Silence. Thank God.

Boom! Boom!

"I think I hate him," Colton muttered, glaring at the window of Harley's stall.

Harley stuck his big black nose out and stretched as far as he could to try to bite Colton again.

"I think the feeling is mutual, my friend. I'm going to take him out and check the creek. The cows are bawlin' awful loud. It's probably frozen again."

"See? This is why I'm totally happy to remain a bachelor for the rest of my life. Girls need stuff all the time. All. The. Time. I can barely take care of myself and my job here." Colton was staring out the open barn door with a faraway look in his eyes. "Totally happy," he murmured again, as if trying to convince himself.

Trigger wasn't doing call-outs on Colton's lie today, though. He had too much on his mind.

Like how the hell was he going to make December special so that Ava could like Christmas again?

TWO

Ava took another long pull of her coffee, which was now ice cold. She made a face of disapproval and went back to organizing the twenty logos she'd come up with for Two Claws Trail Rides. She needed more sleep. Lately, she had been so stressed about getting Trigger and Colton's business off the ground and balancing her own work, she was only sleeping three or four hours a night. She was a financial adviser, newly moved back to Darby, Montana to be with her mate, Trigger, but it meant a whole lot of work trying to get herself set up online to keep her clients.

And with trying to get to know her big brother again, trying to be the best mate she could be for

Trigger, and the work-load, she was feeling the pressure.

The front door creaked open, and she sucked on her coffee again. When she saw her man, the weight in her chest lifted. Maybe it was his smile that eased her tension, or just being around him and feeling safe and loved. He was tall as a mountain and wide in the shoulders, so much bigger than her average-sized frame. He wore his favorite cowboy hat. His go-to blue plaid button-down clung to his broad shoulders, and his worn jeans were sporting a new tear at the left knee. The work boots on his feet were so scuffed she was surprised she didn't see his socks through a hole yet.

When he took off the hat, she went dumb. It happened a lot. It was his routine to remove the Stetson, hang it on the hook by the truck keys, and run his hands through his hair like he was trying to fix it. But it just made it stand up in this messy, sexy way only Trigger Massey could master. The top button of his shirt was undone, and tattoos painted his skin from his neck down into his shirt. She'd traced those so many times now. Those pictures he'd had someone draw on his body were part of his story.

And he had a great story. His newest tattoo was a simple *A* with two claws on either side. It was done in gray-wash ink, right on the side of his neck. It was her favorite. Trigger was now the alpha of the Two Claws Clan, and she was so damn proud of how he'd stepped up for their little make-shift family.

Out of his jacket and hat, he meandered right to her, his boots clomping loudly on the wood floors. He pulled her head against his rock-hard stomach and ran his fingers through her hair. A soft growl rumbled through him, but she knew him well enough that it didn't scare her anymore. His bear was purring just to touch her again. "Smells good," he murmured, looking down at her, his smile easy and sexy on his lips.

"Charmer. I just made toast. I forgot to eat lunch."

The grin faded from his face in an instant. "Ava, that's not good. You'll make yourself sick the way you're going."

"Says the rancher whose work is never done."

"Aw, but when I come in here, when I come home to you, work is done. I'm here. You work all day and into the night. And now you ain't eatin'? Should I be worried? Because I have to tell you that lately, I'm a little concerned."

"One last big push, and things will steady out. When you start doing trail rides, I'll be able to pass the work on to you, other than booking the rides. And I'll have my website up and running in a few weeks, and—"

"Ava. Baby..." Trigger shook his head. "You ain't livin'. You see that right? You never stop, never take a break. And I get it. You have big instincts to take care of your people, and you're working just as hard as me and Colton and Kurt to save this place. You're trying to get us set up, but we're okay. We're holding. Next month we'll do our first trail ride, and we'll get into the routine. I'll hopefully not eat all the tourists, your brother too, and we'll get this place back on track. But for now? I want to see you happy."

"I want to see you happy too, and you told me once that saving this place would do that."

"We will save this place. But I don't want you working yourself to the bone to get us there."

"But...I have twenty different logos to choose fr—"

"That one," he said, jamming his finger at one that looked similar to his tattoo.

"Oh." She frowned. These had taken her all day to put together, and he'd just made the decision in a millisecond. "Okay, well, we need to choose a template for the website—"

"That one's good," he said, pointing to her laptop screen.

"Well...okay, but we need to set up a payment page, and we still need to design brochures to put in the shops in town, take out an ad in the newspaper, get a PO box for the company, and—"

"Woman, put your jacket on."

"What? No, tonight we're going to put a dent in the work and—"

"I ain't askin'," he said, his dark eyebrows arching up high. His eyes were chocolate brown when he was calm, but right now, they were muddy and had gold around the irises. "Put your warm clothes on before I drag you to my truck."

She grinned. "Well, that sounds sexy."

"It won't be sexy when you're shivering in my truck and definitely not riding my dick. You're stressing me out. We need a night away from"—Trig waved his hand around the dining table, which was completely covered with stacks of papers and notes—"this."

"But...what about Colt?"

"He can eat with his damn squirrel. He's been getting on my nerves all day."

"Oh. Well, what about Kurt? He's all alone out there in the barn."

"You mean the barn that's been partially converted to a cabin that's nicer than this one and Colton's house combined? And he ain't alone! He's got Gunner. We can all go one night without eating together. Come on. We're wastin' daylight. You look hot as fuck in those little leggings. I want to take you out, walk around, enjoy the night, eat something other than a quick canned meal. I wanna walk around town and grab your ass and hold your hand."

"It's romantic how you listed grab my ass before hold my hand."

He gave her a devilish smile. "I got plans for us."

"A surprise date?"

Trig eased away from her and made his way back to the coatrack, grabbed his jacket and hat, and flung open the front door. "Meet me in the truck, Ava, before I pry your cute little ass from that chair. Your work day is done."

Newly invigorated by the prospect of an actual night off, Ava squeaked and bolted for the bedroom. The leggings were staying on, but perhaps the coffee-stained sweatshirt needed to go. She pulled on a fitted brown sweater and her favorite tan snow boots and ran for the front door. Purse, jacket, pink hat and mittens, and she was out the door in under two minutes.

Colton was tramping through the snow with his hands shoved deep in his pockets like he was cold, but that was his own fault. Her brother never wore a coat. "Where are you going?" he asked.

She paused at the bottom of the porch stairs and struggled into her jacket. "Into town for a date!"

"Oh, gross," he complained, scrunching up his face. "Wait, what about dinner?"

"Trig said you are annoying and to eat with your squirrel," she called over her shoulder as she jogged to Trig's old two-tone brown Ford pickup.

From Trig's shoulder-heaving laughter behind the steering wheel, she figured he heard her just fine. Colton flipped him off, and Trigger shoved his hand out the open window and returned the bird. Then they were off before she even had her seatbelt buckled all the way.

"I honestly can't tell if you two like each other or hate each other," she said about him and her brother.

"Both. The answer is both."

"Hate," Colton called from behind them. "The answer is hate!"

She would've laughed at her brother except Trigger's face had gone serious and he kept his eyes carefully ahead on the road.

"He doesn't really hate you," she murmured, knowing exactly what was on his mind. Trigger Turning Colton into a bear shifter like himself was never far from his thoughts.

"Maybe he should, though," he said softly.

"If you hadn't Turned him, we wouldn't be here. Colton would've followed me to Alabama, and I would've never had a reason to come back home. And Kurt and his boy would still be with the Darby Clan, miserable, and this—what we're doing—it wouldn't exist. Forgive yourself. Colt has." Probably.

Trig slid his hand over her thigh and squeezed it comfortingly. "You're one hell of a woman, you know that? You're the only one who could ever match me."

Ava snorted and drew her knees to her chest,

cradling his hand against her stomach. "No one can match you, Trigger Massey. You are a giant of a man with a colossus of a grizzly you're trying to control. You fight when you need to defend your honor, you protect the ones you care about, you're loyal down to your marrow, and you work harder than anyone I know. You're a great man, Trig. And a great monster, too." Ava rolled her head against the seat so she could look at his handsome profile. "I'm just trying to keep up."

"If I'm a good man, it's because I'm trying to be. For you."

Well, that slapped a big ol' mushy grin on her face. What power to have sway over a man like Trigger. He was borderline demigod, and she was human, and he was telling her his focus revolved around her, which made her proud.

Great man, great monster.

She was the lucky one.

But she was also the suspicious one, because Trigger turned into the first neighborhood off the main road to town, and he was just coasting down the streets. After the third street, he pointed to a house decorated in red and green holiday lights and said,

"Look at those."

Ava narrowed her eyes at him. "What are we doing?"

"Looking at Christmas lights like a normal couple, and I don't want to hear your bellyachin' either. You can wait on dinner for half an hour more."

He slowly crawled the truck past a house with lights all over the landscaping and a huge blowup snow globe that was raining Styrofoam snow all over a Santa Clause who was holding a beer. The next house had giant wooden story books with the Grinch painted on one and a bed of kids dreaming of sugarplums painted on the other.

And with each house they passed, the discomfort in the pit of her stomach grew. Because now she was scratching at memories she didn't want to scratch. "Can we go now?" she asked softly.

"Why?"

"Because I don't really like Christmas."

Trigger crept to a stop in front of a house that was all done up from the roof to the towering trees in front. White, gold, green, red, and blue lights lit up the entire yard, and three inflatable snowmen sat in front, holding hymn books like they were caroling.

"Why don't you like the holiday?"

"You know why."

Trig sighed and squeezed her hand. "I like Christmas."

"What?" she asked, completely shocked. "You were always so stoic. I didn't think sentimental holidays would be on your radar."

"Every year, me and my dad would make each other a present. Just one, that was the first rule, and the second rule was that we couldn't buy it...we had to make it. And we would make this huge meal. I mean...turkey, stuffing, gravy, ham, Cornish game hens, vegetables, rolls, biscuits, casseroles, mountains of desserts—you name it, we made it. Spent half the damn day in the kitchen, eating as we went. He always joked I was going to eat him out of house and home, but he was a bear shifter, too. He ate just as much as me, and on Christmas day, we would binge eat and watch the parade on TV, then old football games after that. I have good memories."

"And after he passed away? Did you still like it?"

Trigger shrugged up one shoulder and leaned his head back on the headrest. "It was different, but I didn't hate it. I wanted to keep the holiday so I could honor his memory."

Ava felt like crying, but she couldn't explain why. Her heart hurt around this time of year. It had since high school. Since she was sixteen. "I had good memories too, but I think Colton was mostly to thank for them now that I look back. There's these little flashbacks...things that click into place now. Catching Colton wrapping dad's presents to me. Or baking holiday cookies with Colton while Dad sat on the couch drinking and staring at a blank TV screen. Or Dad standing us up for the town parade almost every year, but Colton was always there, making some excuse why Dad had to be late. I used to love everything about the season, and then..."

"Then what?"

"You know what. I remember now. You were there, standing on the edge of the yard, watching us while my Dad pulled away in that old suburban he used to drive, with all our belongings strapped in the back. I was so confused why he'd taken all our stuff, but now I think he took as much as he could pack so he could sell it for gambling."

"Yep," Trig said in a dead voice.

"You think so, too?"

"I know so. I tracked his ass down a month later."

"Wait, you did?" she asked, sitting up straighter. "You saw him?"

"That's one way to put it." His voice had gone hard as stone. "You didn't know it, but I was staying nights at your place while Colton was working those late shifts at the bar. I came in and slept on the floor in your Dad's old room after I thought you were asleep, just to make sure nothing happened to you while Colt was at work. And then I would leave when he got home. Only some nights when I came in, you were in your room, but you weren't asleep yet. I could hear you."

"Hear me what?" she whispered.

"Crying. Your dad did that by leaving, so I went to go find him to drag his ass back. Only when I did find him, I figured out you and Colt were better off without him. He was so far into whatever lifestyle he'd got into, he smelled like the inside of a whiskey barrel and was begging change to go to the races. Beggin' it, Ava. Let that soak in. Your dad didn't care that I was trying to get him to come home and man up and be a father to you. He was worried about how many dollar bills I had in my wallet so he could get another fix on them ponies."

"So you just left him there?"

"No. I waited until he was out of alcohol and sober, then I beat the shit out of him, and *then* I came home. And before you give me crap for whoopin' that old bastard's ass, you should know how hard it was for me to lay on the floor of Colt's room night after night and listen to you crying. All I wanted to do was go in there and scoop you up and fix everything. Fix your life. I wanted to comfort you and take away all that pain, but I had to keep my bear away from you. And it was torture, Ava. Torture, you hear? I loved you then already, and when you have to hear someone you love crying like that? When you can physically hear their heart breaking? Well, it did awful things to my insides, and your dad deserved a fist for every tear you cried over his sorry ass."

Completely shocked, Ava sat there shaking her head, unblinking. "But you didn't kill him...right?"

"No, I didn't kill him. He was spitting a tooth and laughing like a psycho when I left. Said something like, 'They'll be just fine if they have you as their guard dog.' My bear literally wanted to Change and eat him. I probably woulda choked on his gristly ass though, so I decided not to."

Ava snorted, but then she covered her hand over her mouth. This wasn't supposed to be funny. It was wrong to laugh at her mate beating up her dad.

Trigger was biting back a smile now. "It's not funny. I've never been so pissed in my whole life." But his smile twitched bigger.

Ava pursed her lips and stared at him with wide eyes, trying not to laugh.

"Stop," he murmured.

"You beat up my dad for me."

"Yeah, so chivalrous."

"Like you tracked him down and beat him up. Trig, you beat up everyone."

"Well, I can't help it! I don't start it. Well, that one I started, but I mean in general, I don't start the fights." He glanced at her and away. "Not many of them anyway."

"You really like the holiday?" she asked.

"Yeah. And the selfish part of me wants you to like it, too. Not because I want you to make things easy on me during December, but because I like it best when you're happy. I'm addicted to your smiles. They give me boners. I want to get boners all month long."

"God, you're ridiculous. You're sales-pitching me right now, aren't you?"

Trig blinked a few times and pulled an innocent face. "I don't know what you're talking about, but look how pretty those lights are on that house."

Ava heaved a sigh. "If I pretend to be festive this year, will you go easier on me next year? I mean, if I still feel that I just want this month to be over, will you let me be my normal non-elf-self next year? If I try for you this year?"

"Yes."

"Pinky swear?"

Trig put up his pinky, but jerked it away right as she was about to hook hers onto his. "On one condition."

"Seriously? You're going to negotiate?"

"Mmm hmm," he said with a firm nod. "No complaining when we do holiday stuff."

"No complaining to you *out loud*," she countered. Because she was sure-as-shit going to be complaining in her head, and to Colton, and probably Kurt when Trig wasn't paying attention. And maybe to the wishing squirrel, the cows, the horses, any passing birds, and the fence out back.

Trigger grinned and squeezed her pinky with his. "I'm gonna make you love Christmas again."

"Good luck with that," she muttered, feeling irritated as she frowned at the hideous display of gaudy lights on the house across the street. She would never put lights on their cabin. It was a waste of time, and when she was a kid, she was always the one who had to take them all down. It was the least fun chore ever.

Trigger was barking up the wrong tree, in the wrong orchard, on the wrong planet.

Christmas wasn't her thing, and never would be.

THREE

Downtown Darby was decorated in lights, and with the fresh snow on the ground, it was picturesque. It brought back so many memories of her childhood, some uncomfortable, some not, but she'd learned over the last month with Trigger that forgetting the past didn't work. It didn't help not to deal with the uncomfortable parts. They were something she needed to think about, to feel, and to move on from so she could be lighter.

"I helped put up the lights and holiday decorations all down Main Street one time," she muttered as they walked slowly up the icy sidewalk toward Petty's Pizzeria.

"I didn't know that," Trigger said, drawing her mitten clad hand into the crook of his elbow.

"It was for community service hours for college applications."

"Of course it was. Nerd."

She giggled and said, "The outlaw and the nerd. We make quite the pair."

"Our cubs are going to be so confused by their family."

"What? No way, we're awesome."

"A nerd for a mom, and savage monster for a dad, Colt and all his weirdness for an uncle, his damn rabid pet squirrel, and if I can get them to stick around, Kurt and Gunner, two mountain lion shifters in a clan of bears, both of whom live in a barn."

"I see nothing weird about our clan. If we weren't a little dysfunctional, we would be boring. I kind of like that we're always on our toes. Chaos is the spice of life."

Trig snorted and shook his head. "You've been working too much. Your brain cells are shutting down."

Ava shoved him, but he barely moved, the brute, so instead she ended up hurting her wrist. That was the downfall to being mated to a brick house. "Anyway, I stood on a ladder and put up the garland and red ribbons on the street lights."

"That just made me so hard."

"Stop."

"Christmas boner."

Ava caught the giggles and shoved him again, only this time he gave way on account of the ice, and she went with him. With a yelp, she fell face-first toward the ground, but Trig yanked her to him at the last second, and twisted them, protecting her from the fall. She bounced off his stony chest as he landed on his back in the snowy grass next to the sidewalk. There was a second of silence, and then he started cracking up. "A nerd and clumsy. I want a refund. I need a better mate."

"Trigger!" She bit his throat and made chomping sounds. "If I can't have you, no one can." *Chomp, chomp, chomp.*

Trigger was wiggling underneath her from laughing so hard, straight from his belly. He pulled her hair to lift her face away from his throat. She snapped her teeth once. *Snap.*

His dark beard hadn't been shaved in a while, and

it was thicker than usual, but his smile looked so bright and white surrounded by all the dark. "God, I love you, woman," he said in a growly voice.

And right there she had a moment—lying on her favorite person, looking directly into his soft brown eyes that danced only for her, listening to the honesty in his voice as he reminded her he loved her. Thousands and thousands of holiday lights were illuminating the snowy, quaint downtown around them and throwing his face into highlights and shadows. Her handsome man. Her monstrous man. Her outlaw. Her everything.

"I love you back," she whispered, in awe of her life.

His hand went gentle in the back of her hair, and he leaned up and kissed her lips. It was a soft sip that led straight into him pushing his tongue past her lips, over and over in a gentle rhythm. She didn't know how long they lay like that for everyone to see, just...making out like teenagers in first love, but she didn't care. Lately, all she wanted was to heal from everything that had made her chronically angry, and to be happy. Trigger made her want better for her life, so she would be good for him, like he was trying to be for her.

"Get a room," Cooper, the local prop plane pilot, growled from above them. "You're on a fuckin' sidewalk, not a Motel 6."

Smack went her and Trigger's lips as they ended the kiss. With a sigh, Ava rolled off Trigger and onto her back in the snow. "Mr. Cooper, I don't know what you're talking about," she said.

"Yeah, we were only making snow angels," Trigger finished.

Pursing her lips against a giant grin, Ava did her best to keep a straight face while she started flapping her arms and legs in the snow. Trigger was doing the same thing beside her, and Cooper, that old codger, was standing above them glaring at them with his arms crossed over his chest. His eyes were glowing silver, the color of his inner mountain lion, but he wouldn't Change here. Trigger was the most dangerous shifter in these parts, and Cooper was a survivor. He wouldn't take on a grizzly shifter without the Darby Clan here to back him up.

Cooper spat on the ground and stomped away, his boots making deep indentations in the new snow. He was muttering something, but Ava didn't have shifter hearing, and thank God for small blessings, because from the narrow-eyed dirty look Trigger was giving to Cooper's back, he probably wasn't saying very charitable things.

Ava was watching him go when she got distracted by movement and music down the street. The snow was cold against her cheek as she stared at a towering Christmas tree two blocks down. It was all lit up and wrapped in red and gold ribbon, with shiny red ornaments sparkling all over. There was a crowd around it, chattering and sipping cups of something warm, probably hot chocolate if the little stand peddling the stuff by the tree was anything to go by. There was a group of six—three women, and three men—dressed in old-timey garb and singing a carol. It wasn't a traditional holiday song they were singing, though. They were singing a three-part harmony of "Hallelujah."

"Tell me what you're thinking right now," Trigger murmured, up on his elbow, looking down at her.

"I'm thinking it's weird that we're lying in the snow in the middle of town," she lied.

Trigger narrowed his eyes and puckered up his lips like he smelled a rat, so she admitted, "That the music doesn't suck and the Christmas tree isn't ugly. There. Happy?"

"Getting happier. Come on. I can smell the pizza from here, and I'm starving."

"You're always starving," she said as he stood.

"Not my fault. Blame the bear." He offered his hand to help her up, and she took it.

As he hoisted her to her feet, she grunted and said, "A bear that didn't kill Cooper for ruining our make-out session. Trigger Massey, I do declare you are rehabilitated and no longer a monster."

"I thought of at least thirteen ways to kill him in my head."

"Well then, never mind, you are still a monster. I want pepperoni and mushrooms."

"And then hot chocolate by the tree."

Ava rolled her eyes. "Pass. I would rather go back to your truck and give you a BJ."

"Dammit, Ava, don't tease me with that."

She skated away on the ice and laughed maniacally. "It's up to you, Trig. Christmas carols or road head."

"Fuck," he muttered behind her. "Are you going to use that every time I try to make you like the season?"

"Probably. What'll it be?"

Trigger sighed loudly and shoved his hands in his pockets. "Road head. The answer will always be road head."

"Yessss," Ava hissed, pumping her fist one time. Why? Because Ava: 1, Christmas: 0.

This week was going to be a breeze.

FOUR

Dinner had been perfect.

Ava had laughed until her face hurt, and Trig had touched her the entire meal. Sometimes he rested his foot against hers under the table, or rested his hand on her thigh, or put his arm around her shoulders and rubbed her arm with his thumb. Twice he leaned over and kissed her right on her temple like he couldn't help himself. He'd turned her to utter mush by the time the tiramisu and the check came.

But when they left, he grew quiet, and she had this terrible feeling it had something to do with him looking over at that Christmas tree a block down. He turned away and pulled her hand back to the inside of his elbow and went quiet. The smile fell from his face as they walked toward where he'd parked.

No. This wasn't how it was supposed to be when they were about to fool around in the truck. She was coming to realize Christmas really meant something to him. Where she'd clung to the bad memories of her dad leaving a few days before the holiday, Trig had dug his claws into the good memories and released the bad. And now she was going to ruin the rest of his Christmases. That hit her right in the chest.

She didn't want to make Trigger unhappy. She wanted the opposite. She breathed for his smiles. Her heart soared with every laugh he gave her. The Trigger she'd known as a kid had been quiet and somber, and always, always serious. But with each passing day with her, he'd opened up, and she could see...*see*...his life turning around for the better. And she liked to think she was part of the reason for that. But right now, in this moment, as he walked beside her, silent and lost in his own thoughts, he reminded her of the Trigger she'd known as a child. She'd done that.

"Trig?" she asked softly.

"Yeah?" he asked, looking down at her. His smile

didn't even come close to reaching his eyes.

"I'm a little thirsty. And a little cold. I could use something to warm me up."

He stopped walking and squared up to her. "Is this a joke about my dick warming you up?" he asked in the most confused tone she'd ever heard him use.

Well hell, she couldn't help the giggle that bubbled up the back of her throat. "No, for once, I'm not being a pervert. I mean, I could use some hot chocolate."

Trig's eyes lightened to a muddy gold, and his gaze flicked to the giant tree down the street, then back to her. And his slow, answering smile warmed her from the inside out, better than any hot chocolate ever could.

"Okay," he murmured. When he leaned down, the scruff of his beard scratched her face as he kissed her. She cupped his cheeks and kept him for a few more seconds before she eased away.

A flicker of worry dashed though his eyes. "Does this mean no road head?"

Ava burst out laughing. "Who's the pervert now?"

"Me. The answer was always me," he muttered as he followed her toward the tree. "I'm serious. You didn't answer my question."

"Depends on how good this hot chocolate you're about to buy me tastes."

"Fine, I'm making a pit stop then."

"To where?" she asked, frowning at him as she watched him jog across the street.

"To the Gut Shot. I'm getting us some whiskey to put in that drink."

"What? Trig! We can't take liquor out of the bar."

"Woman, I've been arrested for way worse. The cops in this town ain't looking for me to be spiking the hot chocolate. I haven't murdered anyone all day. We're good."

"Well, okay then," she muttered, jogging after him. That was one thing about her outlaw mate. She saw rules and minded them. Trig saw rules and squished them like bugs with his boot. Didn't matter how happy he became with her, he would always do whatever he wanted, and Heaven help whoever stood in his way.

Her man stood at the door to the Gut Shot, holding it open for her like a gentleman, but when she nodded magnanimously and murmured, "Thank you," as she meandered past, he slapped her ass hard enough that she squeaked. Good golly, he was perfect for her.

The devil was in his smile as he pressed his hand to her lower back and guided her toward the bar. The place was hoppin' tonight. This was the local cougar clan's hangout, and Eric, the bartender, slapped his hands on the countertop, threw his head back, and groaned rudely. "No, Hairpin!" he yelled, using the nickname the Clan had given Trigger for his temper and tendency to punish quickly for any slight done to himself or the people he cared about. "I just fixed the damn window from the last time you were in here."

"I swear I won't fight tonight," Trigger said, throwing up his giant, tattooed hands in surrender. "We just need whiskey."

The volume in the place had dropped from an eight to a two the moment they'd walked in, and while Trig was used to negative attention, Ava had always been uncomfortable under scrutiny like this. As she bounced on the balls of her feet, she looked around. The place was basically a biker bar, complete with motorcycle seats on the barstools. Nothing matched, but it all went together somehow from the checkered floors, to the beer-keg tables, to the old green countertops on the bar. The staff had strewn glittery snowflakes along the ceiling and hung strands of red sparkly boas from the rafters. There was even a pitiful, tiny Christmas tree in the corner that was missing most of its limbs. It was leaning at a forty-five-degree angle, and only had one ornament that looked suspiciously shaped like a large, sparkly penis, but it was festive enough.

"I like the holiday decorations," Ava offered to break up the tension.

"Yeah, well, that makes one of us," Eric muttered through a scowl. "Charlotte and Trina put them up. When I told them I was gonna take it down, Charlotte said she would stab my tires with a buck knife. I didn't believe her, so I took all this shit down to get my man-card back, and that wildcat actually did stab my tires. Every damn one of them. And this, Hairpin, is why I ain't even mad that you brought a breeder into Darby. Because women are poison, and Ava is gonna poison your stupid fuckin' clan from the inside out. P. S. thanks for killing half my friends, you—"

"Whiskey!" Trig yelled, slamming his fist on the counter. The volume level in the room dipped to zero. In a cold, steady voice, Trig said, "I just want whiskey, not your life story, and if you call Ava a breeder again, you're gonna join your Clan in Hell. And if you're pissed about me killing your friends, maybe they should've stayed off my land and not tried to assassinate me and the people I protect. Four shots of the cheap stuff so we can leave."

Eric started pouring the booze, but he kept running his mouth. "I know you're hiding that traitor, Kurt. I know it. You're askin' for a second war, Hairpin. A second war, and this time we won't come unprepared. If he thinks him and his cub are safe, he's dead wrong. You don't kill an alpha and survive the rest of the clan. You don't turn your back on your people like that without paying with your life."

Trig stared him right in the eyes and lied smooth-as-you-like without a single hitch to his voice. "Kurt left two weeks ago, and we ain't seen him or heard from him since. Fuck off with your threats. And if he did ever decide to come back, you would have to come through me. Y'all didn't manage it the first war with an entire damn clan. I wish you big luck coming into my territory and trying to hurt something that's mine again. You're lucky I'm not hunting every one of you down, one by one. Don't think I haven't obsessed over it either. The only thing keeping you alive right now is the lady you're callin' names. Best show Ava more respect." Trigger offered Eric an empty smile, and his eyes blazed bright gold when he pointed to Ava. "You're still breathing because of her."

Ava had been busy eating handfuls of snacks from the nut bowl on the counter, and her mouth was full. When Trigger pointed, she froze, her head thrown back with a handful of peanuts ready to dump into her maw. Slowly, she tightened her fist around her food and gave Eric a bright smile. "I'm making Trigger not so murdery. You're welcome."

Eric frowned and yanked the bowl of nuts away from her. Rude. He replaced it with a Styrofoam cup of whiskey and jerked his chin at the exit. Whooo, his eyes were such a bright silver they were hard to look at.

"Happy holidays," she said cheerfully as she followed Trigger toward the front door.

"I hate y'all," Eric called.

"See you tomorrow," Ava sang over her shoulder.

She definitely was *not* coming back tomorrow, but she felt like annoying Eric, because it sucked every single time she got called a breeder in this town. She and Trig were in love, not paired up in some emotionless match. It was a degrading term, and though she never showed anyone it hurt to be called that, inside it was like little slashes on her heart when that word was thrown at her.

"Fuckin' breeder," muttered some idiot with two beers in his hands as they passed.

With barely a hitch in his step, Trigger drew his massive fist back and slammed it into his face. Probably broke his nose from the definite crack she heard and the subsequent groans afterward. Her man was quick as a cobra strike, and furthermore, why did the people of this town not learn their lessons? He'd fought damn-near every one of them and won. Why did people keep testing him?

She hadn't been a big fan of blood before coming back to Darby, had always grown nauseous when she saw it, but then the war had happened, and she'd seen and done things that changed that. She was in the Two Claws Clan now and mated to a man who didn't take shit from anyone. Her life would probably be painted in red. She shook her head sympathetically at the village idiot who had tested Trigger. He was standing with his legs splayed, shock in his glowing eyes and both hands over his bleeding nose. "Maybe put an ice pack on it?" she said helpfully.

"You swore you weren't gonna fight!" Eric yelled.

Trig was standing there holding the door open for her with one hand and the cup of whiskey with his other. Two of his knuckles were bleeding. Cool as you like, he said, "I lied."

"Thank you," Ava told Trig primly as she made her way through the exit.

Trigger gave her a sexy-boy wink and said, "Anytime."

"Well," she said cheerfully as she aimed her boots toward the giant Christmas tree, "at least you didn't kill anyone."

"Christmas miracle," he muttered, shaking out his hand as they walked.

"This is actually fun!" she said, taking the cup of whiskey out of his hand to sip. "I haven't even thought about work all night."

Trig blew onto his closed fists, trying to warm them up, then wrapped his arm around her and kissed the top of her head. "Good. Ava, you know you're safe, right?"

"Yes. Why did that come up?"

"I just don't like anyone from the Clan making threats in front of you. I don't want you getting scared off."

"I know it's weird for a human to say, but I'm kind of getting used to the shifter stuff. You guys live by different rules."

"Yeah, no rules."

"Not true. You live by an honor code and go to blows when you are crossed. You don't tattle or let offenses pass. You get pushed and you react, and then you move on."

"Nobody in this town moves on. There will be a million of those little fights until the day I'm in the ground. I was fine with that before you came back to Darby, but now I wish it was different. I wish things were steadier, or that I was more accepted in this town for your sake. So you can go to the store without me tagging along like your watch dog." He was getting serious again, and that was a party foul, so she took a healthy shot of whiskey, which felt like lava going down her throat, and then stopped at a vender in an elf costume selling Santa hats. She pulled one off the cart, took off Trigger's cowboy hat, and then replaced it with the red number with the snowball on the top.

"Do I look fuckable?" he deadpanned.

"Gasp! We should dress like Santa and Mrs. Clause and diddle on a bed of cookies!"

"God, I love your brand of weird."

"Thank you." She pulled a headband with light-up reindeer antlers onto her head and gave Trig her most seductive look. Lowering her voice, she murmured, "Ride me, Santa."

Trigger let off a single, bellowing belly laugh, and Ava turned to the vendor and asked, "How much for these two?"

The man answered, "I'm closing in five minutes and things are slowing down, so three bucks apiece and they're yours."

"Sweet." Ava wrestled enough cash out of her wallet, handed it to the vendor, and then hesitated when he told her, "Merry Christmas."

Clutching her twinkling antlers, she forced the words past her lips. "Merry Christmas," and then she walked with Trig toward the tree. "I'm so Christmasy right now," she said softly.

"You're doing so good," he complimented her.

The carolers were singing a slow song, and it was truly beautiful, so she stopped to watch them. It wasn't ten seconds later that Trigger turned her in his arms and started slow dancing with her right there in the middle of the sidewalk with people around them. The Trigger from childhood wouldn't have ever wanted that kind of attention, but Trigger, the man, didn't care what people thought. Only what she thought, and this was so sweet, swaying back and forth to pretty acapella music, looking up into his gold eyes, absorbing that all-important smile that curved his lips. Her heart was beating hard and fast against her sternum, and when she melted against him and rested her cheek against his chest, she could hear his beating just as fast.

She still didn't like Christmas. It still wasn't her thing and never would be. But tonight was special.

Trig was happy, she was happy, and all was merry and bright in her little world.

FIVE

"I liked last night," Trig murmured from behind her in the dark before dawn.

"Mmm?" she asked sleepily.

"I said I liked last night."

With a happy sigh, Ava snuggled back against her big-spoon. And he was a giant spoon. The man was six-foot-three and his feet hung off their bed. He'd turned the heater on in their room because she'd gotten so cold, and it seemed he couldn't go back to sleep. She squinted one eye open at the alarm clock. They still had an hour before he needed to get up to feed the cattle and tackle the hundred chores he had to do around the ranch today.

"I'm gonna plan adventures for us," Trig said.

"What kind of adventures?"

"I want to do something fun every day from here until Christmas. Something for you and me mostly, but sometimes for you, me, Colton, Kurt, and Gunner."

Ava drew his arm tighter over her hip and kissed his hand, right at the base of his thumb. Even in the dark, she could trace his tattoos. She'd memorized them all. "Like dates?"

"Like new traditions."

"Will any of the traditions be illegal?"

"Probably."

She giggled and murmured, "We could call it the Seven Days of Outlaw Christmas."

"I like that. Let's count it down. Like an advent calendar, but instead, it's a list of things we could do every year."

"Hmmm," she hummed happily. He was making a game, and she loved those.

Trigger brushed his fingertips across her lips, then to her jaw, neck, and the tip of her shoulder. She was only wearing panties, which is why she'd gotten cold in the first place.

"Remember when you first came back to Darby,

you said you wanted a baby reindeer and baby goats so you could dress them in pajamas and they would be your hairy babies and you would make them social media pages?"

"Mmm hmm," she said, utterly distracted by what his fingertips were doing. He was writing something on her hip, over and over, and she was trying to read it just on feel alone.

Ava Massey. Ava Massey. Ava Massey.

Well, now she was awake. "Are you writing your last name on my first name?"

"Maybe."

Huh. She relaxed against him again and couldn't help the grin that took her entire face. "It has a ring to it."

"You're mine now. You know that, right?" Trig gripped her hips and rolling his own against her back.

Ava let off a shaking breath and arched back against him. She slid her hand over her shoulder and gripped the back of his neck as he plucked at her sensitive earlobe with his lips. His fingers dug into her skin as he rocked against her, and she could feel him so easy like this. How hard and big he was. He was only wearing a pair of sweatpants, and his abs were flexing against her back with every stroke. He took his time, revving her up, teasing her, getting her ready before he took her.

His fingers drifted under the lacey edge of her panties before he slid them down her legs. Trig was smooth, like he'd taken lessons on removing panties, but she still lifted to make it easier for him. They only made it to her ankles before his hand was back on her hips. When he pushed against her, she could feel his dick between her legs, touching the wetness he'd made there.

"You gonna take it for me?" he murmured. When Trig eased back, she could feel him right there.

"Yes," she gasped as she writhed back against him, silently begging.

The swollen head of his hard cock slid into her for just a second before he pulled back.

"Please," she pleaded.

"God, I love when you beg for it."

"Please, please, please," she whispered mindlessly as he pushed into her another inch. She spread her legs, urging him to stop the torture.

"Good girl," he whispered against her neck, and then he gripped her hips hard and pushed into her, deeper, deeper until she took all of him.

"Oh my gosh, Trig!"

He eased back slow, then slammed into her. Eased back, slammed. Eased back, slammed. There was a snarl in his throat now, and she was totally gone, her focus completely on how he felt inside of her. His body had been made for her. Perfect match, perfect fit.

Ava had been gripping the pillow in front of her, but Trig slid his fingers from her hip to her hand. "Feel us."

He guided her hand between her legs so she could feel them. Her fingertips brushed his slick cock sliding in and out of her. He was so hard. Trig pushed her hand down, putting pressure on her clit. Moving with him, she kept her hand there, gasping with every stroke. So close, and he was pushing into her harder and deeper now. Faster. Faster. He was close, too. The bear inside of him always gave it away. He got growly. Trig pulled her knee farther up, spreading her legs more, and then his hands were on her hips again, jerking her back against him as he bucked into her.

She cried out as she came, and two strokes later,

Trig groaned, and his dick throbbed hard inside of her. Once, twice, three times, he was filling her. Sexy noises in his throat, helpless ones in hers, and her orgasm went on and on. He drew every one from her until she lay there twitching, completely sated. He didn't leave her right away. Instead, he hugged her up tight and rested his face against the back of her neck. He stayed inside of her, connected.

"You make me better," he said in a deep, gravelly voice. "You make everything better. Make me try harder. Make the bear try harder. I got so lucky the day you came back to Darby. I never thought I would have a single easy day in this life, and then you came in and changed everything. You're the best thing that ever happened to me, Ava, and someday I'm gonna put my last name on you. You can have everything. Anything you want. All of me." His lips brushed the back of her neck gently. "I'm yours."

Tears burned her eyes. He'd come so far, yes, but so had she, because of him. He didn't realize what he'd done for her, or how big a difference he'd made in her life. And not just now, either. She hadn't known it at the time, but he'd watched over her when they were kids, too. He'd always been hers. And she was just realizing she'd always been his as well. She'd felt so alone for so long, but she never really had been. She just hadn't been paying attention.

And now look at her life. By witnessing his growing happiness, it was fueling her own. And she was pretty sure this was how it was supposed to work. Love was supposed to be like this. He thought he was the lucky one that she'd come back to Darby, but she'd been living filler years. Forgettable years. She'd been wasting her life, and now everything was in such sharp focus because of him.

He didn't realize it, but he'd saved her in a lot of ways. Trig had earned her loyalty.

"I want to chop down a Christmas tree for the house," she whispered, her heart aching and soaring all at once. This was a huge moment of growth for her, and it wasn't an easy one. "I swore to myself I would never celebrate Christmas again when my dad left. I swore I would never get attached to anything again. Not any person, not any home, and not any tradition. But…" Ava swallowed hard and found the courage to finish. "With you, I want to try."

Trig let off a sigh as though he'd been holding his breath. "Day six. Chop down a tree for our cabin." He rolled out of bed.

Ava tried to follow, thinking he wanted to get up for breakfast, but Trig pressed her back down in the dark and tucked her under the blankets. "Go back to sleep, mate."

"What are you going to do?"

"I need to Change. What happened at the Gut Shot last night riled up the bear, and he's been loud all night. I don't like when people threaten you, or call you names. I don't like it when they test us. I'll Change while you sleep, and then I'll gather the Clan and we'll find a tree when you're ready."

"Trig?" she asked as he made his way to the door.

Moonlight streamed through the window, highlighting his naked body in blue shadows. "Yeah, Ava?"

"I don't like that you have to Change alone. Sometimes I wish I was a bear shifter too, so I could be in the woods with you."

She could hear him swallow hard. "If you saw what I did to Colton, and what he went through, you wouldn't wish for the bear. Sleep, Ava. I'll be back soon."

Ava lay in the dark, under the warm blankets, in

the breeze from the heater, until the front door clicked closed. And then she slid from bed and made her way to the window. The sky was clear, and the half moon and stars illuminated the yard.

Trig tromped in the ankle-deep snow until he reached the tree line, and then he turned toward her as if he could feel her watching him. He stood tall and proud, muscles rippling, the tattoos on his shoulders, arms, and torso stark against his pale skin, his breath frozen in front of him, his eyes so bright she could see them glowing from here. Beautiful monster.

She knew what he would do before he even started breaking. He was going to show her what the bear did. Show her the pain on his face. He was going to remind her it was a curse to be a shifter.

And as his body ripped apart and reshaped into a massive brown bear with a roar so loud it shook the house, she blew a breath on the window, then drew a heart for him and colored it in with the tip of her finger.

Because man or beast, he owned her heart.

And no matter what, he always would.

SIX

"Now?" Gunner asked in his little, squeaky three-year-old voice.

"Son, you've asked that a dozen times, and the answer is still no. She ain't ready yet. Girls take longer to—"

"I'm ready!" Ava called, bustling down the front porch stairs with the basket of warm, buttered blueberry muffins. "I was making breakfast for us."

Trig, Colt, and Kurt stared at her like she'd grown a triple head.

"What?" she asked as she leaned down to give Gunner one. He was a bundle of excitement and currently touching every muffin, trying to pick one.

"You cooked for us," Colton said suspiciously. "But you hate this time of year. I thought you were going to stand us up, but you made muffins like Suzy Homemaker. Who are you and what have you done with my sister?"

"In the traditions with Dad, I never made us muffins for breakfast. He was allergic to blueberries. We're doing this one different."

Trigger was grinning from ear to ear with an ax thrown over his shoulder, looking like a hot, tattooed Paul Bunyan. Kurt was frowning at his son, Gunner, who was still picking up muffins and putting them back to choose the one with the most blueberries, and Colton was now on his tiptoes, looking hopefully into the basket of pastries.

"Miss Ava, I have to tell you something!" Gunner yelled at an uncomfortable volume.

The boys all hunched their shoulders, and Ava thanked the heavens she didn't have their sensitive hearing.

"What is it?" she asked.

"Mr. Colton teached me to draw a picture."

"A picture of what?" Kurt asked.

Gunner pointed to a snow pile near the cabin.

Squinting, Ava walked over to the drift and yep, that was a little yellow pecker he'd drawn while peeing. Fantastic.

"Goddammit, Colt," Kurt groused.

"Okay, bright side," Ava said, because she loved bright sides and could find them in just about any situation. "Gunner's picture is way better than Colton's big one," she said, pointing to the shaky, giant pee-nis her stupid brother had drawn beside Gunner's.

"Where are you going?" Trig yelled out.

Ava turned around just in time to see Gunner the Runner disappear into the trees. Kurt shoved Colton so hard he almost fell. "Never talk to my kid again, you delinquent asshole." And then he went jogging after his son.

"What did I do?" Colt called after him.

Trig walked toward the tree line, muttering something that sounded suspiciously like "the cubs of this Clan are gonna be so screwed up."

But she was human and didn't have that good of hearing, so she was probably mistaken.

Munching on a muffin as she went, Ava made her way after the boys and hoped they waited for her near the tree line. She'd tried to keep up with them in the woods for about ten minutes on their first hike, then gave up. They all had speed and agility on their side, and long legs, even little Gunner, while she, the puny human, was clumsy and tripped every thirty seconds and got stuck in the snow drifts. She was training them to go slower and wait for her. So far it wasn't going that well, but someday she would have them whooped into shape. Probably.

She ate three muffins before she found the rest of her clan. It wasn't that hard because they were all yelling at each other about a hundred yards away from the house, each arguing they'd found the perfect tree.

"This one is tall and full," Colt argued.

Looking nonplussed, Kurt cocked his head and insulted it. "It's skinny as a bean pole."

"Well, the cabin is kind of small," Trig said, staring at the emaciated pine tree thoughtfully.

"I like that one!" Gunner said, pointing to a short, squatty tree with full branches. It would take up most of the living room with girth like that.

"That has my vote, too," Kurt said, trying to snatch the ax from Trig's hand.

Her mate yanked the handled blade away and pointed it at Ava. "She's Queen of Christmas this year. Ava picks."

"Well, I like that one," she said, pointing to the winner. It was the most pitiful tree she'd ever seen, even more so than the one in the Gut Shot. The branches were bare in patches, making it look like it had mange, half the needles were brown, and the tree had taken damage to the top half of it at some point and was now growing at an angle.

"That is the saddest tree I've ever seen," Kurt muttered.

"Don't be mean to it! I think it's cute. I'm going to name it Kevin."

"Well Kevin is hideous." Colt jammed his finger at it. "You're gonna take the choice away from a little three-year-old kid for *that*?"

"I don't think he minds," Trig deadpanned. "Gunner's too busy eating a snowball."

Kurt looked down at his hungry son and snorted.

"Thirsty," Gunner said around a bite of the white stuff.

"Why this one?" Colt asked.

"Because we used to spend hours searching for

the perfect tree with Dad, and I want to do our traditions different. I want to pick the trees no one else would. It reminds me of us. Outcasts. None of this town would bet on us, but we're still here, and I think we're pretty cool."

Colt blinked slowly. "You just compared us to an ugly tree."

But Trig had already pulled the ax back to slam it into the trunk, and Ava just smiled. Of course, he would understand. Trig always had her back, just like she had his.

He made quick work of it and then took her hand as he started dragging it toward the house like it weighed nothing at all. Kurt and Gunner had a snowball fight while Colt complained about everything—the tree, the snowball that hit him in the ballsack, the cold weather, how Trigger's horse had escaped again, about how he would never let a girl tell him which tree to chop down, and about how he'd eaten all the rest of the muffins and was still hungry—basically life in general. Her brother had never been much of a morning person.

And as for Ava...well, her nose might have been hurting from the chill in the air, but her cheeks hurt from smiling. She wouldn't say it out loud to them, but she loved these crazies. And this morning had been fun. Humming under his breath, Trig wasn't even showing any soreness from his Change, and he smiled every time he looked down at her, which was often. He kept looking at her lips, like he was just as enamored with her smile as she was with his.

And once they were in the house, they decorated that misshapen little tree with a box of old scuffed-up ornaments that Trig had dug out of the back of the bedroom closet. It was loud the whole time, mostly with arguing, and some with Gunner's excited yelling. But Ava just absorbed it all. She didn't mind the chaos this morning. Why? Because this was the first time she was decorating a tree in a decade, and it wasn't horrible. It was fun because of the people she was with. Because of the Clan, her little make-shift family. Because of Trigger.

And oh, that tree wasn't cute. Trig had to superglue a cardboard cut-out star to the crooked top because the old store-bought star-topper wouldn't stay on and Colt had broken it in three pieces trying to force it anyway.

But so what? Kevin looked as good as a little

outcast tree could look.

He was perfectly pathetic.

And somehow, someway, as she looked around at her little rag-tag crew...this place felt even more like home.

SEVEN

7 Days of Outlaw Christmas

Day 7: *Christmas fight with asshole in bar, whiskey in hot chocolate, dance to carol singers. Ava's smiles today: 38.*

Day 6: *Chop down tree. Ava picked Kevin, the ugliest tree in existence and compared it to the Two Claws Clan. It's perfect. Ava's smiles today: 51*

Day 5: *Put lights on house. Took me and Kurt and Colt six hours to figure out why the lights weren't working. It was one stupid bulb that was out. Next year please God let us have enough money to buy new strands of lights. Ava's smiles today: 59*

Day 4: *Watch Christmas parade. Two more Christmas fights. Not my fault, for once. The Warmaker aka Colton-who-has-to-get-in-a-fight-over-his-hotdog-not-being-made-correctly started both of them. I finished them. Ava yelled a lot. Colt ate twelve hot dogs and hoarded the candy they threw off the mayor's float in the parade, and then he pegged two cougar shifters with the candy, got drunk at the Gut Shot, and we had to drive him home in the bed of the truck because he was getting on my damn nerves. Ava's smiles today: 78.*

Day 3: *Baked Christmas cookies and decorated them. I made eighteen perfect snowman cookies, and Ava and Colt made twice that many shaped like dicks. They used skin-toned frosting and white sparkle sprinkles at the tips, and now we have to eat them. Dicks. We have to eat dicks. Ava's smiles today: 89*

Day 2: *Christmas movie marathon day. I thought this was going to be horrible on account of all three dominant male shifters shoved in my tiny cabin watching chick-flic holiday movies. It was fine though, because Ava didn't make us watch the mushy shit. She picked a couple funny ones and made us caramel popcorn and apple cider and we ate a dozen of the frosted dick cookies. None of us even Changed in the* *front yard and bled each other, and I'm counting that as Christmas miracle four-hundred. Today on the couch, I noticed Kurt favoring his injuries though, and when I asked, he wouldn't show me. He turned on his Clan and killed his alpha to keep Ava safe, but he got bad hurt. I owe him sanctuary, but I don't think he's healing right. He wants to leave as soon as he's able to defend his cub, but truth be told in this journal, where no one will ever read, for Christmas I wish he and Gunner would stay.*

Day 1*: It's Christmas eve today. I'm running ragged trying to keep up the ranch and spend the quality time with Ava that she deserves. This morning she said we need to do a work day. She's falling behind, too, but we only have one life, and I want to live it. She thinks we aren't doing anything for the holiday today, but I'm meeting up with Cooper for a special delivery, and then I'm coming in at lunch to make her present. I spent almost all the rest of my coffee can savings on the materials. As long as she doesn't pop into the barn today, I'm in the clear. It's so much less than she deserves, but I hope she likes it. God, please let her like it.*

Trig put the cap back on the pen and closed the journal. He hadn't written in the thing for years, but he wanted to write it all down so they could do the same again next year.

And the year after.

And the year after that.

Because he could see a change in the woman he loved. It was subtle but steady. Her smiles were growing each day, numbering more and more. He was counting.

She was starting to like Christmas again.

And because of it, the holiday was becoming more special to him, too.

EIGHT

Day one, Christmas Eve, and Ava had tricked Trig into having a work day. Muahahaha. She had worked for a few hours, caught up on what she could, and now she was in Colton's cabin, ignoring his half-rabid wishing squirrel, Genie, who still seemed to hate her. Genie was currently sitting in her cage with her hands wrapped around the bars, glaring at Ava. She hadn't seen the angry critter blink in a very long time.

Slightly disturbed, Ava forced her gaze away from the poofy-tailed rodent and went back to mashing the clay into the shapes she wanted. She'd really thought this would be easier because she'd taken a sculpting class in college, but making a motorcycle ornament out of clay was quite possibly the hardest thing she'd ever done in her life. There were so many tiny pieces. She looked at the picture of the Road Glide she'd taken again. It was Trig's newest motorcycle, sitting in the storage shed, waiting on warm weather so Trig could hit the open road again. Riding was his freedom. And he'd also said his tradition with his dad had been to make each other a present each year, so here she sat, trying to replicate an ornament of his favorite motorcycle out of children's clay.

Another wave of nerves took her. She hadn't done Christmas presents in a long time, and what if he didn't like this or thought it was lame?

Another half an hour, and she finally scratched onto the back the year and *Our First Christmas - T & A*. She giggled when she realized their initials could be mistaken for the acronym for titties and ass. Perfect. The ornament needed to be cooked in the oven to set and dry, so she did that. She ignored the fact that her ornament could look like either a motorcycle with handlebars or a dog with its head sticking out the car window with his ears flying back. Surely, Trigger would guess it was a motorcycle. Hopefully.

The door blew open, and in with Colton drifted

snow flurries. "Holy hell, it's cold as balls out there."
Once again, her brother wasn't wearing a jacket, just
a blue jean button-down, a cowboy hat, and a pair of
threadbare jeans that were ripped at the knees. His
arms were loaded with grocery bags.

"What's that for?" she asked, pointing to the
shopping spree he'd just done.

"My Christmas present to the Clan. I blew all my
savings on this, but whatever. I'm cooking for
everyone on Christmas day. Trigger told me once that
he and his dad used to cook all day and watch football
reruns and eat until they almost puked and that
sounds a lot like Heaven to me, so...we're doing this."

"Aww!"

Colt made a clicking sound behind his teeth as he
passed on his way to the kitchen. "Don't aww me. I'm
doing this for selfish reasons. I like to eat."

"But you picked Trigger's tradition with his dad
to make it special for him. I know you did. Act tough
all you want, Colton Nathanial Dorset, but you take
care of your people, and Trig is your people."

"Don't make it sound weird. You just girled all
over something I wanted to do. I got four pounds of
bacon, Ava! Don't tempt me to return this stuff. My

damn mouth was watering the whole time I was shopping. Leave your mushy girl shit in your head. It weirds me out."

She hid her emotional smile by giving him her back and making her way to the oven to removed her little motorcycle ornament. Her brother was tough and funny, but he could also be thoughtful and sweet, and she liked that side of him.

"Hey, Colt?"

"What?" he asked in a grumpy tone as he put entire bags of groceries into the fridge like the total bachelor that he was.

Before Ava could change her mind, she strode right up to him and hugged him up tight. She had to stand on her tiptoes to squeeze his neck. "I'm really glad I get to spend Christmas with you."

Colt had frozen the instant she'd hugged him, but a few moments later, he sighed, expelling the tension, his shoulders relaxing, and he hugged her back. "I'm really glad, too, Sis. I didn't ever think we would get a second shot at this. We'll make it good, okay? We'll take it back."

"What do you mean, take it back?"

"I mean we gave Dad power for way too long. We

let the things he did and the decisions he made affect how we lived our lives. And he don't care, Ava. He's not sitting around pining for us, or worrying over what he did. He moved on the second he pulled away from our house. Now it's our turn to move on. You did really good despite what he did." He patted her back and lowered his voice, which had gone thick with emotion. "I'm so damn proud of you."

Tears spilled onto Ava's cheeks as her face crumpled. God, it felt so good to hear those words from him. She hugged his neck tighter and made water spots on his denim shirt with her crying, but it couldn't be helped. She wasn't a crier, but he'd opened the flood gates. It was crazy how kind words could change the path of a life. How having someone who was uplifting in your corner could mean the difference in success or failure.

She had succeeded in school back when she was a kid because Colton had sacrificed more than she would ever be able to understand, just so she could stay steady and make the grades. And now she was succeeding as an adult because her brother supported her in improving the quality of her life. And maybe Colt was right. Maybe it was high time she forgave Dad and took that power back. Not for Dad. Fuck him. The forgiveness was for her. It was an *I love you* to herself. It was the belief that she deserved better than wrestling with her past for the rest of her life. She did deserve better, and so did Trig, and so did Colt.

So okay.

Forgiveness granted.

As she stared up at the rafters, hugging her brother, tears staining her cheeks, she let the hurt go. Oh, it would come back in bursts for a while as she was daily reminded of her past. But this was her time to accept she was going to work on her and move forward to a damn good future, not look backward to the past.

She didn't know what Christmas would bring, but she was now certain of one thing.

Between her brother, Kurt, Gunner, and especially, especially Trigger...

This was going to be the best Christmas ever.

NINE

Ava followed her nose into the kitchen, thinking Trigger would be there making the breakfast that was filling up the entire house with the scent of cinnamon and sugar. She was surprised to find Colt standing over the stove instead, though. He was frosting some raisin cinnamon rolls, and on the couch, playing a Grinch-themed monopoly game, were Kurt and Gunner.

"Smells good," she muttered, pulling a newly frosted pastry from the pan.

"The only reason I'm not slapping your hand away is because it's Christmas. That is your present," he brother said without skipping a beat on frosting.

"It's hot," she said as she switched the breakfast roll from hand to hand to save herself from burns. "Where's Trigger? Out with the cows?"

"You could say that," Kurt said from the couch.

"He's doin' a game!" Gunner said, smashing two game pieces together repeatedly like they were fighting.

"A game?" she asked.

Colt licked icing off his thumb, then grabbed a red envelope from the counter and slapped it into her empty hand.

"What's this?"

His only answer was to stare at her and shove an entire cinnamon roll into his mouth. He couldn't even shut his mouth while he chewed. Boys were gross.

Ava took a bite of her breakfast, set the remaining part on a napkin, and rinsed her hands, her attention never leaving the envelope. On the front was drawn a sad, crooked Christmas tree and a heart with the letter *A* inside of it.

Ava opened it, and inside was a holiday card with a picture of a snowman in a top hat. She pulled open the card and read.

Ava,

You made a deal and gave me this year to help you like the holiday again. I hope I succeeded, because it's been the best December of my life. You make every month the best month of my life though. I have one last surprise adventure for Day 0, Christmas. I'm nervous, so go easy on me. Go put on your jacket and your warmest snow boots. It's cold this morning. And when you're all cute, because I know you'll be wearing your pink mittens and beanie and looking so pretty, go look in the barn in the stall next to Harley's. Don't get too close to Harley though. He is a Grinch and his attitude has been horrible lately. Don't get bit. I can't wait to hold you.

Yours always,

Trig

Ava read it twice because it made her feel fuzzy and good inside. *I can't wait to hold you.* She knew exactly what that relief would feel like. It was the same every time he touched her after working all day away from the cabin.

Shoving the card back in the envelope, she made her way to Kevin, grabbed the little wrapped present she'd made, and went to the front door in a rush. She dressed warm, and slipped her boots onto her feet, right over her fleece leggings. She put the card between her teeth to free up her hands to zip her jacket as she made her way through the front door. When she turned to check that the big metal door swung all the way closed and latched, the sunlight glinted off the house numbers. She called them wishing numbers because they repeated. 1010, and there were bear claw marks on the wood all around it. Trig had made those when he was out of control of his bear, but he didn't do that much anymore.

I love my life, she thought and touched the number with her mitten-clad pointer finger. *I wish for Trig to have the best day.*

She turned and jogged down the porch stairs, shoving the holiday card into her coat pocket. The barn was a hundred yards off, on the other side of the clearing. It had been painted red at some point, but most of the color had chipped off to expose the gray, aged wood underneath. She'd always loved this old barn. In front, Queenie, her white, winter-furred nag, was leaned against the fence, sleeping with one back hoof propped up, her breath steaming in front of her face. Ava's boots made crunching sounds in the crisp snow, and the song of bellowing cattle filled the clearing. The furry beasts were gathered near the barn, probably waiting on Trig to spread out hay for them.

She grunted as she pushed the sliding barn door open. Inside, dust motes swirled in the air, and the scent of animals hit her. It was much warmer in here. In the back were the living quarters for Kurt and Gunner, and at the front were two rows of stalls with different colored horses sticking their faces out expectantly. Every stall was full this morning except for one, the second on the right, the stall near Harley's. The sound of jingling bells rang prettily from it. Something was moving in there.

Slowly, Ava made her way past Harley's stall, careful to stay out of biting distance, and with only a moment of hesitation, she gripped the cold iron of the handle and slid the heavy door open.

What she found inside stunned her into stillness. A tiny brown and cream, lanky-legged animal stood inside, staring back at her with big, blinking brown eyes. It didn't have antlers yet, but she knew what it was immediately.

A baby reindeer.

Trig had gotten her a reindeer. Slowly, Ava shut the door behind her and dropped to her knees by the little critter. Soooo cute. He startled when she touched him, and she had to scoot to it again on her knees closer. He finally allowed her to pet him, which made her cry like a total wiener. Trig had really gotten her a reindeer. There's no way he would've separated it from its mom, so maybe it was a little orphan, kinda like her. She was going to take such good care of it. Trig had listened when she'd told him what she wanted. When she had first come back to Darby and was falling in love with him, she'd mentioned this, and he'd made it happen. For her.

Overwhelmed, she scooped the baby into her arms and sobbed, shoulders shaking. Trig had fixed her broken pieces before today, and now he was filling her heart with joy just because he could. Its little hooves bumped against her legs, but he didn't try to get away. The baby was patient, or maybe he'd been hand-reared until this point and liked cuddles. He wore a collar of jingle bells, and there was a small green card attached to it. Sniffing, she plucked it off and opened it clumsily. It was hard to read through the tears that blurred her eyes, and her voice shook as she read it aloud in shock. "Marry me."

The door slid open loudly behind her, and there he was—her mate. Her Trig.

He wore his favorite cowboy hat, but took it off and set it against his chest as he dropped slowly to one knee beside her.

Ava lost it. Shoulders shaking, she thought no girl had a right to this much happiness in one moment. She cradled the reindeer to her chest as her face crumpled.

Trig pulled out a simple gold band. The color matched his eyes.

His voice was thick and full of emotion when he said, "Ava Dorset, I've loved you since we were kids, and I never thought you could be mine. I don't deserve you, but I'm gonna work to make you happy. I told you about a tradition I had with my father, where we made each other a single gift each year. You deserve so much more than this, and someday I will get a pretty diamond, but this year, this is what I can do. I bought the gold raw, and I made the ring. You are the heart of this place. You're my heart. This is the easiest question in the world for me because I can't imagine my life without you. I want every minute with you. I want to grow old with you. I want to see you holding our cubs. I want to take care of you and build my life around you. You. Make. Me. A better man." He swallowed hard, and his eyes were rimmed with moisture. "Ava Dorset, will you marry me?"

Kneeling there in the hay, she was crying too hard to answer. He'd busted her heart wide open, and thank God for him, because she'd lived a half-life before he'd kissed her that first time. Not anymore. He was offering her something she'd only dreamed about—infinite happiness. Crying too hard to get a single word out, she nodded.

"Yeah?" he asked, his dark eyebrows arched up high. "Yeah?" he asked louder, a smile spreading across his lips.

"Yes," she croaked out. "I'm yours."

Trig slid the ring on her shaking finger and then palmed the little reindeer's stomach to lift him and set him aside in the hay. "Sorry, Norman," he murmured. "I need to hug my lady," he murmured, squeezing her tight against his chest.

She couldn't breathe, but she couldn't find it in herself to care. Over Trig's shoulder, she saw Kurt standing in the open stall door, holding Gunner. Colt was beside them, leaned against the frame, a soft smile on his face, raw emotion in his eyes. He nodded like, *You done good, girl.*

The hardest thing she'd ever done was to open up to a man. To Trigger. But she'd let him make her brave, and look what had happened?

He'd given her everything.

A home where she felt safe and warm.

Her brother back.

Kurt and Gunner.

A Clan.

This rough-and-tumble group of boys would always have her back. Of that, she had no doubt, and they'd earned the same fealty from her.

He'd given her a little reindeer named Norman and a life she could be proud of. A life that fulfilled her.

But most of all...very most of all...Trigger had given her his heart.

And that was the best Christmas gift of all.

Want more of these characters?

For the Love of an Outlaw is the first book in the Outlaw Shifters series.

For more of these characters, check out these other books from T. S. Joyce.

For the Heart of an Outlaw
(Outlaw Shifters, Book 3)

For the Heart of the Warmaker
(Outlaw Shifters, Book 4)

For the Soul of an Outlaw
(Outlaw Shifters, Book 5)

About the Author

T.S. Joyce is devoted to bringing hot shifter romances to readers. Hungry alpha males are her calling card, and the wilder the men, the more she'll make them pour their hearts out. She werebear swears there'll be no swooning heroines in her books. It takes tough-as-nails women to handle her shifters.

She lives in a tiny town, outside of a tiny city, and devotes her life to writing big stories. Foodie, wolf whisperer, ninja, thief of tiny bottles of awesome smelling hotel shampoo, nap connoisseur, movie fanatic, and zombie slayer, and most of this bio is true.

Bear Shifters? Check

Smoldering Alpha Hotness? Double Check

Sexy Scenes? Fasten up your girdles, ladies and gents, it's gonna to be a wild ride.

For more information on T. S. Joyce's work,
visit her website at
www.tsjoyce.com

29478749R00207

Made in the USA
Lexington, KY
31 January 2019